Amy Cross is the author of more than 200 horror, paranormal, fantasy and thriller novels.

OTHER TITLES
BY AMY CROSS INCLUDE

American Coven
Annie's Room
The Ash House
Asylum
B&B
The Bride of Ashbyrn House
The Cemetery Ghost
The Curse of the Langfords
The Devil, the Witch and the Whore
Devil's Briar
The Disappearance of Lonnie James
Eli's Town
The Farm
The Ghost of Molly Holt
The Ghosts of Lakeforth Hotel
The Girl Who Never Came Back
Haunted
The Haunting of Blackwych Grange
The Haunting of Nelson Street
The House on Fisher Street
The House Where She Died
Out There
Stephen
The Shades
The Soul Auction
Trill

1722

THE HAUNTING OF HADLOW HOUSE BOOK TWO

AMY CROSS

This edition
first published by Blackwych Books Ltd
United Kingdom, 2023

Also available in e-book format.

www.blackwychbooks.com

CONTENTS

1722

PROLOGUE

THE HOUSE STOOD EMPTY and quiet, as it had stood empty and quiet now for more than three decades.

As late afternoon light streamed through the window, bringing with it the shadows of bushes and trees outside, the old study revealed layers of dust covering every surface. No living thing had entered this house for many years, not so much as a fly had breached any of the rooms, and the only sound came from the rustling of the nearby forest. Somewhere in the distance a crow called out, swiftly answered by another, but these sounds of life could have come from another world. This was a house that – having been sealed for so long – seemed now to almost exist in another world.

Up on the landing, more dust drifted through a shaft of sunlight that had broken through one of the windows. Here too the house remained deserted, save for one thing. At the top of the stairs, on the curve of the banister, there rested one pale hand.

CHAPTER ONE

17th March 1722...

THE STREETS OF LONDON were cacophonous, filled with the sound of carriages and voices and the growing pains of industry. Anyone watching from afar would be unable to pick out much order in this chaos, and would instead see a streaming mass of people and horses rushing in every conceivable direction, pushing against the walls of buildings as if to test just how far they might go.

Somewhere in this hysterical crowd, one particular man threaded his way between heaving bodies. Unlike many of those around him, Samuel Butler knew exactly where he was going.

***

“He doesn't even speak English,” Toby Wallace murmured as he sat at his desk in the office of Saville and Wallace, a few streets back from The Strand. “Can you comprehend that? We have a king on the throne who doesn't even speak our language?”

“This is what we fought for, apparently,” Samuel pointed out with a faint, wry smile. “Better a foreigner than a Catholic, or at least that's what I was told.”

“Meanwhile the population has become overrun by a craze for bad living,” Toby continued, sighing for what must have been the hundredth time since he'd sat down. He turned and looked over at the nearest window, as if searching for confirmation of his fears. “Great rivers of alcohol run through parts of this city, turning the faces of our workers red and puffy. How are we still to be considered a serious country? How are we to be considered a force? Why, have we not invited our own invasion?”

“I do not mean to change the subject,” Samuel replied cautiously, “but I confess that I am anxious to learn more of this opportunity you mentioned. In your letter of last Tuesday, you suggested that a position might have opened up beyond the city."

"Indeed," Toby said, nodding sagely before looking down at the documents spread out across his desk. "It is exceedingly rare for something like this to occur, but a chance has come up for a good man to oversee the transformation of some land. Have you ever heard of Cobblefield?"

"Should I have?"

"Not really. It's a village down in Kent. Anyway, the long and the short of it is, my company has come into possession of a tract of land that might be suitable for any of a number of purposes. The area is rather underdeveloped, as these countryside locations tend to be. Ordinarily I would not go to such extremes in my attempt to turn the place around, but for two factors that make this particular situation different. First, I foresee the potential for a rather healthy financial return. And second, by the grace of God, this land comes with a property."

"Oh?" Samuel shifted a little in his seat. "What kind of property?"

"Well, there's a house there," Toby told him. "I haven't seen it myself, but by all accounts it's fairly new, it was built thirty or so years ago by someone who then rather lost the plot. Literally and figuratively. So, you see, if you were to move your young family down there, you would have ample lodgings and the deed would be passed to you, and you would be able to pass it on later to your own family."

"I see," Samuel replied. "And this house..."

"It's a little way outside the village," Toby warned him, "which is a fact that comes with positives as well as negatives. You would be away from the bad influences of the world, which I know concerns you as a father. Then again, your walk to church each Sunday would be a little longer than you might be used to." He paused, watching Samuel's face carefully for any sign of a reaction. "But you *would* be going to church, I assume?"

"The thought of not doing so," Samuel told him, "never crossed my mind."

"Then it would seem to me that there is an arrangement to be made here," Toby said, allowing himself as much of a smile as ever crossed his face. "What do you think, young man? Are you up for a change of scenery?"

***

"And what kind of house is it, exactly?" Rose asked as she turned to her husband.

"I suppose it's a house like any other," Samuel replied, standing in the cramped kitchen of their little home in the north of London. "It must surely consist of walls and floors and a roof. And windows too, I'd wager."

"Don't try to be smart with me," she said skeptically. "If you're proposing to move us all down to Kent, then I want to know what we're getting ourselves into. Toby Wallace is widely regarded as one of the most miserly men in all of the country, so what is he letting us move to this house without charging us any rent?"

"Well, I'd be undertaking certain work for his company," Samuel told her, "and in return, as well as a salary, he has offered us a long lease on the house. With the understanding that I shall be responsible for certain improvement works, of course." He paused, before stepping over to her and placing a hand on the side of her arm. "This is what I have wanted for our family for many years now," he continued. "London is changing, Rose, and I worry that it is no place to raise a family. Meanwhile, I myself am in my forty-fifth year and I confess that I tire of so much hubbub and madness. Do you not feel the same way?"

He waited, but for a moment Rose seemed reluctant to reply.

“It's the smell that gets me,” she said finally.

“The smell?”

“Oh, it stinks!” she continued, her eyes open wide with horror. “You must have noticed, Samuel! Have I not commented on this before? The more people flood into this city, the worse the stench, and I can only imagine that it is going to get much worse. But how can anyone tolerate such a thing? Is it not possible that in another decade or two, men will start to drop dead because of the wretched stench of one another?”

“You might have a point.”

“I do not believe that people are supposed to live in this manner,” she continued. “Everyone is rushing about, bumping into one another, and I fear that soon we shall run out of air! When so many men are standing shoulder to shoulder, how can we be sure that there will enough air for all of them? Why, I feel a man could suffocate outdoors, purely because those around him are breathing the air that he needs! That could happen to you!”

“It will not,” he replied, “but this is all the more reason for us to take Toby Wallace up on his generous suggestion. We can start afresh, Rose, and build new lives in the beautiful, bucolic English countryside. I know we've both heard some rotten things about Kent, but it can't be as bad as people say, especially inland. It's not as if we'll be in any of the rougher seaside towns like Dover or Deal or Crowford. We'll be far from all of that, and we can start our lives afresh." He waited for her answer. "Please, Rose," he added. "I could insist, but instead I will only make this decision if you agree. Wallace thought me a fool for that position, but I cannot help myself."

Rose opened her mouth to reply, but for a few seconds she seemed genuinely undecided.

"This house had better be habitable," she warned him finally, with just a hint of a smile. "If we get there and find that it's a pigsty, I won't let you hear the end of it."

"That won't happen, I promise," he told her. "So you agree?"

"I agree," she replied, "although I fear that this will not be as easy a change as you're suggesting. For one thing, we have both lived in the city all our lives, we are not accustomed to life out there in the countryside with all that mud and rain and... insects. There will be insects, will there not? And sheep?"

"There might well be," he told her, "but I shall do my best to guard you from them."

"And then there is the other matter," she said cautiously. "After all, it is not merely you and I who must deal with this change. There is also -"

Before she could finish, the back door opened and a younger girl walked in, barely in her early twenties and covered from head to toe in soot.

"That is no job for a woman!" she protested as she set her basket down. "I was laughed at by all the boys on the street!" She wiped some of the soot away from her face, and then she furrowed her brow as she saw the smiles on the faces of her parents. "What?" she added. "Why are you looking at me in that way?"

CHAPTER TWO

"WHERE IS EVERYONE?" PATIENCE asked several weeks later, as she walked with her parents along the country lane that led out of Cobblefield. Looking around, she saw only rolling fields. "Is something wrong? Why are there no people out here?"

"You saw people in the village," Samuel called back to her. "You saw their houses, and their inn, and the shops that some of them run. You saw them getting on with their daily tasks. They live there, and then the fields are where they keep their livestock and grow their crops."

"So all this land is empty?"

"It's not empty," he replied with a smile. "It's just being used differently. And without places like this, our cities would be even worse, for we would receive none of the crops that are being grown in places such as Cobblefield."

"But it's so quiet," Patience pointed out. "I think this is the first time in my life, at least as far as I remember, that I don't hear voices shouting at one another. In fact, I think my ears are still ringing with the din of London."

"That will fade," her mother told her. "At least, I hope it will, for I hear the same thing. A kind of echo that still will not go away, reminding me that London is still out there somewherc, albeit all those many miles away."

"How many miles are we from London?" Patience asked her father. "Is it more than ten?"

"I believe it is more than fifty," he told her.

"More than fifty?" This news clearly surprised her, and she walked along in silence for a few seconds as she tried to comprehend this fact. "I suppose that explains why I can no longer hear any of it."

"We have arrived," Samuel said suddenly, stopping at the point where a rough road branches off from the lane, heading into the forest. "Our new home is at the end of this route, somewhere beyond those trees. By my reckoning, we only have another half hour to walk before we reach it." He turned first to his daughter, and then to his wife. "Are you not beside yourselves with excitement?"

"I'm beside myself with dread at the thought of how dirty the place must be," Rose said, rolling her eyes before setting off past him. "Come along, there's no point dawdling. Let us set eyes upon the place!"

***

The journey took more like three quarters of an hour, but finally they reached their destination. Emerging from the forest path at the edge of a small river, the three of them stopped as soon as they spotted the low-walled garden with its arched metal sign, and the house itself a little way further off.

"Hadlow House," Patience whispered, taking a step forward as she looked up at the sign. "Hadlow?"

She turned to her father.

"Who or what is Hadlow?"

"The man who had the house built, I would assume," Samuel replied, making his way over to join her and then looking all around. "It is much as Toby Wallace described it. There is the big old oak tree he told me we would find, and over there is the actual house, which certainly looks strong and sturdy enough. Indeed, I was expecting something a little more ramshackle, so I might even venture to say that I am pleasantly surprised."

"There's a lot of mud," Patience pointed out, looking down at her feet for a moment before glancing toward the river. "That thing doesn't look very fresh. I can't imagine that many fish enjoy swimming in such murky water."

"There's time to fix all of that and more," Samuel replied, placing a hand on her shoulder and making a point of taking a big, deep breath. "I see great potential here, although there will be a lot of work to do first. I shall start by familiarizing myself with the house and its grounds, so that I might determine where best to start. Patience, you are about to see a very different side of your father. I am going to be working much more with my hands, and generally getting dirty in a very practical manner."

"It's so cold here," she told him. "The trees seem to shield much of the house from the sun, and there's a stillness that seems born of that."

She looked toward the oak tree, and after a moment a faint shiver ran through her body.

"There's an atmosphere here, too," she added. "It's unlike anything I have ever felt before, but I feel as if this entire clearing is..."

She paused, struggling to think of the right phrase, before finally turning to her father again.

"Holding its breath," she suggested. "Does that make any sense at all?"

"You are merely struggling to adapt to life outside the city."

"I don't think it's that," she replied. "Father, I know how important this is to you, but I feel as if there is something untoward here. Something that should not be. I don't know how to explain that sensation, it's just something in my bones. I thought that coming out to the English countryside would make the world feel natural again, certainly more natural than the filth of London, but instead I am gripped by an incomparable strangeness."

"That's the spirit," he chuckled, patting her on the back before stepping over to the gate and pulling it open, causing the hinges to creak loudly. "You are alive to the change that we are experiencing, and that can only be a good thing. I think you're going to love living out here, Patience. Once you get used to the place, you're going to wonder how any of us ever survived in London at all!"

Patience opened her mouth to ask more questions, but her father was already marching away and she quickly realized that there was no point trying to temper his enthusiasm. A moment later, she turned as her mother wandered over to join her; she could already tell that her mother did not share her father's excitement at the vast scale of the challenge that lay before them all.

"Do you feel it?" Patience asked. "Am I imagining things? Am I being a fool? Mother, tell me honestly, does this place feel natural to you?"

"Nothing feels natural to me these days. I fear I have enough dirt from the city hiding in me, to last for a very long time indeed." She took a moment to look around, and nothing about her face suggested that she was overly excited about what she saw. "It's a little more isolated than I expected, and you're right that it's rather cold. I must speak to your father and possibly having some of those trees taken down so that we get more sunlight here. And as for that river, I must warn you not to go into it, for it appears to be rather dirty."

"That is what I thought," Patience told her. "I suppose we must trust Father, though. He always knows what he's doing."

"I don't see that we have very much choice," Rose muttered, as she saw her husband examining the old oak tree a little more closely. "Those men'll be up from the village soon with our things, so we'd best get ourselves ready. There'll be a lot of work to do as we settle in, and I'm afraid I'll need your help." She began to make her way toward the gate. "In my experience, a house like this is capable of throwing up some real surprises."

Left standing alone, Patience knew that she should follow her parents, yet instead she chose to hang back. For some reason that she couldn't quite determine, she felt strangely reluctant to go anywhere near the actual house itself. She looked at the building's dark windows, and although she saw no sign of anyone inside she still couldn't shake the feeling that she was in some way being watched. She told herself to put such foolish ideas out of her mind, and she had certainly never before entertained such strange ideas, yet the sensation persisted and – if anything – began to grow more and more prominent in her mind, until she caught herself checking the same windows repeatedly in order to search for a face.

"Patience!" Rose called out, waving at her. "Come along! For better or for worse, it's time to take a look inside this place!"

"It's a big house!" Samuel shouted. "You're going to love it!"

"I'm sure," Patience murmured uncertainly, before setting off after them.

She told herself that all her fears were

unfounded. Still, she couldn't shake a growing sense of unease as she passed under the metal arch and stepped for the first time into the grounds of Hadlow House.

CHAPTER THREE

"THERE'S SO MUCH MORE room than we're used to!" Samuel called out excitedly from somewhere far off in the house. "Rose, do you see how big this place is? I dare believe that one could swing a cat in here and not hit any of the walls!"

With her parents having gone on ahead to explore Hadlow House, Patience stepped more cautiously into the hallway. She was immediately struck by the cold, slightly damp air, and by the smell of dust mixed with wood. Stopping to look down at a table by the wall, she ran a fingertip against the surface and found that there was a thick layer of dust. She walked over to the foot of the stairs and looked through an open door, and she was surprised to see that the next room was filled with a healthy amount of furniture. A desk was over by the window, there were books on the shelves and a chair had been left in the corner. Until that moment, she had not considered the possibility that the house's previous owners might have left behind any of their possessions.

"How strange," she whispered, before turning and looking up the stairs.

Somehow the landing above held a particularly ominous presence, and Patience had to admit that she felt no great desire to go up there. Indeed, the entire house somehow even stiller and quieter than it had seemed from outside, to the extent that it felt less like a home and more like a graveyard. Stepping over to another door, Patience looked through and saw what appeared to be some kind of sitting room. She made her way to the fireplace and reached down to touch the metal in the hearth, which of course turned out to be entirely cold. At least the hearth had been cleaned, which she supposed meant that there was one less job that had been left needing to be done.

"What do you think?"

Turning, she saw a silhouetted figure in the doorway. For a moment the room was too gloomy for her to make out any features, but her eyes adjusted to the darkness and she saw her father smiling at her.

"Isn't it magnificent?" he continued, stepping into the room, his shoes tapping loudly against the exposed wooden floorboards. "I confess that I was careful to not oversell the prospect to you and your mother, but I scarcely believe that I need to show such restraint. Is this house not a completely different world to our stuffy, tiny little home back in London?"

"It is certainly unlike anything I have ever seen before," she admitted, struggling a little to come up with much enthusiasm. "I confess that the countryside is not quite how I imagined."

"Your mother is already complaining about the dust," he said, lowering his voice a little, "and I understand such a sentiment, but I believe it is important to look beyond the immediate state of the place. Think of how it can be once we have turned it into our own."

"It's not our own, though, is it?" Patience replied. "Can this Mr. Wallace gentleman throw us out whenever he wishes?"

"I have secured a one hundred year lease," he explained, "that can be easily extended by those who come after us. Really, there is no need to worry in that regard."

"Those are generous terms," she said,

stepping past him and heading to the window. Looking outside, she saw the front garden and the oak tree. “One cannot help but wonder why such generosity has been advanced. Father, exactly how long has this house stood empty?”

“Three decades. A little more.”

“Why?”

“I'm not sure what you mean.”

She turned to him.

“Why has it stood empty?” she asked. “It is indeed a fine house, as you yourself have noted, and the position near the edge of the village is excellent. So why has such a house been left unoccupied for all these years?”

“I'm not sure that I recall,” he said, a little unconvincingly. “That doesn't really matter now, though, does it? What matters is that we are here, and that we are going to turn it into our home. Why, it remains Hadlow House for now, but I wouldn't even mind asking Mr. Wallace eventually if we might change the name to Butler House. Don't you think that sounds fun?”

“I fear you are getting ahead of yourself, as usual,” she countered.

“If I am,” he replied, “it is only because I am glad that we have escaped the madness of London. That place is only going to become busier and more overwhelming as time goes on." He paused, before walking over to her. "You don't *really* mind leaving the city, Patience, do you? You were always complaining about the dirt."

"That I was," she admitted with a smile. "There is dirt here too, of course. But it's different dirt, and perhaps not so harmful." She hesitated, but she could tell that her father was seeking reassurance, so after a moment she leaned up and kissed him on the cheek. "Thank you for arranging for us to move here," she said, even though she still had her reservations. "I am sure that eventually we shall all mark the change as a great success."

***

"It's a good-sized kitchen, and that much is certain," Rose said a short while later, as she sorted through some old pans that she'd found in one of the storage rooms. "Almost too big for me, I'd wager, but let's not tell your father about that. I shall just have to up my game."

"I can't get over how much room there is," Patience replied as she leaned into what appeared to be some sort of pantry. There was even another door at the far end, no doubt leading into yet more storage space. "How can just three of us rattle around in such a house? There is room for five times as many people!"

"Oh, we'll fill it up, alright," Rose called through to her. "Especially your father. Once he gets to work, he'll have all sorts of things dragged up here."

"I'm sure you're right," Patience whispered as she looked at the empty shelves in the old pantry. For a moment she felt as if the room was somehow staring back at her, but she quickly put such thoughts from her mind and headed back into the kitchen. "I still don't entirely understand Father's work here. What exactly does this Mr. Wallace gentleman want him to do?"

"Your father is to oversee the land and other interests of some people in London," Rose explained. "Beyond that, I confess that I too struggle to quite define the detail, but I'm sure he'll be busy. I hope so, at least, for I really can't handle having him running around the place and getting in my way."

She turned to her daughter.

"Which means, by the way," she added, "that you shall have to pull your weight. You won't have as much free time as you're used to."

"I do not recall living a life of leisure in London," Patience replied, raising a skeptical eyebrow.

"Nevertheless, things will be different now that we live in such a big house," her mother continued, turning to attend once more to the pans.

Patience rolled her eyes.

"And there's no need to roll your eyes at me," Rose added.

"How did you even know?" Patience protested, before spotting her mother's smiling face staring at her, reflected in the window. "You don't need to talk to me as if I'm a child," she continued. "I'm fully capable of pulling my weight, as you put it. Indeed, I should positively hate to think that I ever lay around relying upon the work of others. You know, sometimes I think that you mistake me for someone else entirely."

"So are you ready to work right now?"

"I was thinking I might go outside and attend to some matters in the garden," Patience told her proudly. "I've already noticed several spots where some serious, back-breaking work is required, and I certainly don't need directing toward such things."

"You have some good ideas," Rose said, before turning to her, "but actually, there's one task that I need you to complete in the house first."

"Name it," Patience replied defiantly. "I

shall shirk from nothing."

"Well," Rose continued with a faint smile, "there was one job you were very good at back in London, on account of your rather slight stature." She paused, as if she was greatly amused by what she was about to ask her daughter. "And as it happens," she added, "I was in the front room earlier and I noticed that there seems to be a blockage affecting the fireplace."

CHAPTER FOUR

"COUNTRYSIDE," PATIENCE MUTTERED UNDER her breath as she took a moment to adjust her position in the darkness, "city, wherever. It doesn't really matter. I still end up doing the same -"

"Do you see anything?" Rose called out from down below.

Sighing, Patience looked up toward the higher part of the chimney. So far, she'd managed to shimmy to about the halfway point, using her hands and knees and back; she'd done this job hundreds – if not thousands – of times back in London, and her diminutive stature meant that she'd been called upon to clean chimneys even when she'd hoped to outgrow such a filthy task. When moving to Cobblefield, she'd hoped that those days might be over, yet now here she was once again halfway up a chimney and covered in soot while searching for some kind of blockage.

"I don't think this has been cleaned in a very long time!" she called back down to her mother.

"But no-one has lived here in a very long time," Rose replied, "so it has not been in use."

"You wouldn't tell that from the state of it," Patience continued, as she reached out and placed her left hand on a section of brickwork. "I know it's not my place to have an opinion on such things, but I can't help thinking that some aspects of this house's construction are rather lacking."

"Have you found a nest?" Rose asked.

Patience looked back down. She could just about make out a patch of light at the bottom of the chimney's narrow shaft, and a bobbing shape that she assumed must be her mother staring back up at her.

"Not so far," she explained, "but I've still got a way to go. Just give me a minute or two."

"There has to be something up there," Rose told her. "The second I tried to light it earlier, smoke entered one of the bedrooms upstairs."

Supposing that there was no point replying until she had more to tell her mother, Patience focused instead on climbing higher and higher. Her progress was slow and painful, and she truly felt as if she was too old for this job, but she also felt determined to prove her worth. And then, as she inched even higher, her hands felt an unusual, uneven section of brickwork in the midfeathers section of the chimney stack.

Stopping to investigate further, Patience peered at the damage and saw that her initial assessment had been correct: the midfeathers was a link of bricks that should separate the different flues within the overall chimney stack, yet her the bricks had been damaged. Indeed, ass she took a closer look, Patience realized that she could just about see through into one of the bedrooms. In that case, she reasoned, there was little surprise that errant smoke might find its way into the upper floor.

"There's damage!" she called out. "Father will have to look at this! You must not light anything in this chimney until it has been fixed! I can't imagine what might have happened here, but either something attacked the hearth in the bedroom or whoever built this thing should never be commissioned for the construction of another house ever again!"

She waited, and then – hearing no reply – she looked back down the chimney. She could still see a hint of light at the bottom, but there was no longer any sign of her mother.

"Did you hear me?" she shouted. "Mother?"

Again she waited, and after a moment she let out a sigh of frustration. Evidently her mother had decided that she had better things to do than assist in the clearing of the chimney, and Patience told herself that she should perhaps not have expected any better; she turned to look at the damaged bricks again, wondering how such damage could be caused in the first place, and then she broke into a sudden coughing fit as she felt soot entering the back of her nose.

Adjusting her position so that there was no risk of falling, she continued to cough for a couple of minutes. Once she felt that she'd managed to clear the obstruction, she reached down and unhooked the brush that had been dangling from a hook on her belt. She supposed that she might as well clean away some of the extra soot around the damaged area of the flue, even if this would inevitably bring about another coughing fit.

She began to brush the soot away, but a moment later she spotted movement on the other side of the gap in the midfeathers, as if somebody had just walked past the fireplace in the bedroom.

"Mother?" she called out, a little confused. "Is that you?"

She waited for an answer, but no answer came.

"Mother, there's a lot of damage in here," she continued. "You'll have to fetch Father and get him to decide what to do next. In fact, I'm surprise that neither of you noticed this before. If -"

Before she could finish, the figure

reappeared, stopping in front of the gap.

"Oh," Patience sighed, "so you *can* hear me. Mother, I can clean a chimney but alas I lack the ability to restore the brickwork. Is Father still inspecting the river? I fear there is limited need for me to remain up here. I might as well climb back down soon."

The figure remained in place, and after a few seconds Patience realized that this woman was wearing a dark gray dress, whereas her mother's clothing had been more of a brownish color.

"Mother?" she said cautiously, wondering why and how her mother might have changed so quickly. "What are you doing in there?"

She adjusted her grip on the bricks again, and a moment later she heard the sound of her father laughing somewhere outside the house. Furrowing her brow, she wondered who he was with, but a moment later she heard a second laugh, and a shiver ran through her bones as she realized that this second laugh was not only strangely familiar but also completely impossible.

"Mother?" she whispered.

She momentarily looked up at the top of the chimney, trying to work out how she could have seen her mother in the bedroom and heard her somewhere outside the house. When she looked through the gap in the midfeathers again, she was shocked to see that the strange figure had now disappeared. Her parents were still laughing outside, and now she found herself wondering exactly who else might be in the house. She peered more closely at the gap, and at the bedroom on the other side, yet now there seemed to be nobody there at all, and she found herself wondering whether she might have imagined the whole thing.

"I'm coming down," she said under her breath, as she began to maneuver herself for the descent. "There's no -"

Suddenly a hand reached through the gap in the brickwork and grabbed her by the throat, slamming her against the inner wall of the flue. Letting out a shocked gasp, Patience immediately lost her grip on the bricks; her feet slipped and she reached out desperately to find some way to hold on. At the same time, she could already feel a cold, dead hand tightening its grip on her throat, squeezing tight as if someone was determined to choke the air from her lungs.

"Mother!" she gasped, reaching up and trying to pull the hand away from her throat. "Help me!"

No matter how hard she tried to force the hand's fingers back, she found that its grip was too strong. She tried instead to push the hand back through the gap, hoping that this might help her to escape, but nothing worked. Barely able to breathe at all now, she realized that the hand's grip was firm and absolute, and that she had no way of breaking free. Straining every sinew, she twisted first one way and then the other, but now she could feel the steely anger of the hand as it squeezed ever tighter, and after a few seconds she realized that sharp, ragged fingernails were starting to cut through her skin.

"Please," she gasped, "what -"

"Patience?"

As soon as she heard her mother's voice coming from below, everything changed. The hand suddenly released Patience's throat, leaving her to tumble down the shaft. She reached out to try to catch herself, but she succeeded only in slowing her fall – just a little – until she landed with a thud and a cry in the hearth at the bottom. As a thick cloud of dust and smoke filled the air, she rolled off the hearth's heavy metal grill, and finally she looked up and saw her mother's startled face.

"Patience," Rose stammered, clearly completely shocked by the sight of her daughter, "what were you doing up there?"

CHAPTER FIVE

"AND I HAVE ALREADY told you," Samuel said as he stood in the kitchen, "there is nobody else here in the house. Do you think that your mother and I would not have noticed such a thing?"

"I'm not a liar," Patience replied, struggling to hold back the tears that were threatening to gather in her eyes. "Why won't you believe me?"

"Obviously *something* spooked you up there," Rose pointed out, "but you were in a dark, cramped and unfamiliar space."

"You might be surprised to learn this," Patience told her, "but once you're up a chimney, they all look more or less the same from the inside."

"It was perhaps a badger," Rose suggested.

"A badger?" Patience replied incredulously.

"There are badgers in these parts, Samuel,

are there not?"

"I am sure," he replied. "I have heard that they are a scourge for some of the local farmers."

"So a badger, or something similar, perhaps attacked you," Rose said, "and in the chaos and confusion, you momentarily lost control of your senses."

"A hand reached through and tried to strangle me," Patience replied. "That was no badger."

"It might have seemed to change its shape in the darkness."

"Do badgers have hands?"

"I have not seen one with my own two eyes," her mother told her, "and nor, I believe, have you."

"Let us not quarrel," Samuel said calmly. "Patience, no good will come from fevered tales of strange hands. I have inspected the hearth in the bedroom upstairs and it is as you described, so at least I know what needs to be fixed. We shall have to avoid using that chimney and rely upon the other, until such time as I have been able to get someone out here."

"But -"

"And let us speak no more of strange sights and sounds in the house," he added firmly. "Such fears have a way of multiplying. It is better to nip the whole thing in the bud, and to accept that although we might never determine precisely *what* happened, there is no danger to us now. Can we all at least agree upon that?"

"We can," Rose said.

Patience opened her mouth to reply, before sighing as she realized that there was really no point arguing. Her parents had a frustrating tendency to close ranks whenever the family discussed any important matters, with Patience always left to feel like a child whose opinions were of no worth. She knew what had happened in the chimney, she could even still feel the soreness on her neck, but she no longer had the strength to argue. Besides, she knew that her claims sounded utterly bizarre, and she had to admit that she was constantly trying to work out whether she might have somehow imagined the whole incident.

"Then that is settled," Rose continued. "No more silliness."

Sitting in silence, Patience couldn't help but feel supremely foolish, but once again she knew that she simply had to bend to her parents' wills.

"Patience," Rose added, "would you help me clean the kitchen? I must have it ready for the morning."

"Of course, Mother," Patience said obediently, getting to her feet. "Please, tell me exactly what you wish me to do."

***

Several hours later, as she lay in bed, Patience found herself reliving the incident in the chimney over and over again. Although she'd tried desperately to convince herself that the whole thing had just been in her head, she was unable to quite shake the sense of that strange hand gripping her throat.

Rolling onto her back, she reached up and touched the side of her neck. Her mother had dismissed the cuts as just injuries sustained in her fall, yet Patience knew that they'd been caused by ragged fingernails digging into her flesh. She winced as she felt a flicker of pain, and she felt sure that in some way her skin remained a little colder than it should be, as if the chill of the hand was not entirely gone from her own body.

And she thought of the calmness. There had been nothing frantic about the hand's grip; instead it had seemed almost cool and calculated, filled with a kind of icy determination. Whoever had owned that hand, they had clearly mean to kill, and Patience couldn't help wondering that she might try again.

A moment later, hearing a bumping sound coming from somewhere downstairs, she immediately sat up. Her heart was pounding now and after just a couple of seconds she heard the same sound again, as if something or someone was moving around downstairs. At the same time, she knew that her parents had retired several hours earlier and that neither of them had since risen from their beds. She told herself that this was her first night in an unfamiliar house, and that most likely the property was merely shifting in the cold night air, as such properties were liable to do.

Hearing another bump, she scrambled to her feet and made her way to the door. As she looked out onto the landing, she caught herself wondering whether this was something entirely new, or whether previous occupants of the house – whoever they might have been – were also sometimes disturbed in the dead of night.

Once a few silent seconds had passed, Patience stepped out from her room and made her way to the top of the stairs. She briefly considered disturbing her father, before realizing that she'd do better if she investigated the source of the noise for herself. Making her way down the stairs, she tried to avoid making too much noise, although as she reached the bottom she found that the very last step let out a faint creaking sound beneath her foot. She hesitated, worried that she might have woken her parents, and then she looked through into the book-lined study.

She waited, but she saw and heard nothing.

After a moment she turned and crossed the hallway. She looked into the front room, and she saw the spot where she'd so ignominiously landed after tumbling down the chimney. She waited, but yet again she heard absolutely nothing, and she was already starting to think that she should perhaps head upstairs. Realizing that she should probably be thorough, however, she walked past the stairs and looking into the dining room, and then she made her way quietly into the kitchen and stopped once again to glance around.

The kitchen of Hadlow House, she had to admit, was exceedingly large, running from one side of the house to the other. Indeed, she wondered whether the kitchen itself might be almost as large as the tiny house that she and her parents had occupied back in London. There was certainly a lot more room out in the countryside, and she was starting to understand why some people seemed to love this lifestyle so much. As she walked across the kitchen and headed to the far window, she realized that perhaps the overwhelming silence of the house – and of the entire area – was meddling with her thoughts. She looked out at the darkness and realized that this might be the first moment of true silence that she had ever experienced in her life.

And she liked it.

At that moment, as if to mock her, a single bump rang out from the other side of the kitchen. She turned and looked, half expecting to see someone standing in the shadows, but there was no sight of anyone. Still, too many of these bumps had now followed one another, to the point that she felt sure there had to be a cause. At the same time, she once again thought back to the hand that had grasped her throat in the chimney, and she felt more certain than ever now that it *had* been a hand and that she hadn't simply imagined the whole thing. She was sick of not being believed by her parents and while she intensely disliked the idea of someone else hiding in the house, part of her wanted to find such a person if only to prove that she'd been right all along.

Yet how could another woman be lurking unseen in the house, and why – having gone to all the trouble of remaining hidden – would such a woman then reveal herself in such a shocking manner?

Heading to the other window, Patience looked out once again. She saw only darkness, and she heard only silence, and she was starting to think that – no matter the mystery – she was going to achieve no resolution while standing in her nightgown in the kitchen during the middle of the night. With that in mind, she turned to go back to the hallway, only to freeze as she suddenly saw the moonlit face of a man staring in at her through the window.

Before she could stop herself, Patience Butler screamed.

CHAPTER SIX

"NO, IT'S FINE," PATIENCE said the following morning, as she followed her father along another narrow street in sun-drenched Cobblefield, "I don't expect you to believe me. I don't expect *anyone* to believe me ever again."

"I looked at the ground outside the window," Samuel replied, with the tired tone of someone who was sick of explaining basic facts to an imbecile, "and -"

"And there was no sign of a disturbance," she continued. "Yes, I get it."

He stopped and turned to her.

"I am an imbecile," she added, with a strange hint of pride. "It's quite simple. I'm a foolish girl who imagines hands and faces at the drop of a hat. I shall try to cease such behavior, of course, but

I cannot promise that I shan't later imagine flying horses or pigs walking on their hind feet or all manner of absurdities. But it's okay, Father, because I shall keep them all to myself. After all, the last thing I would want to do is embarrass you."

"You are no imbecile, Patience," he told her. "Quite the reverse. Sometimes I think you are too intelligent for your own good. Whoever ends up marrying you is going to have their hands quite full."

"What if I don't *want* to marry anyone," she suggested.

"Now this conversation has become ridiculous," he replied, before glancing over his shoulder and looking toward the butcher's shop on the corner. "I must go and speak to a gentleman in there," he added. "Patience, can you wait out here and try not to get into any trouble?"

"I'll do my very best," she said sarcastically, before turning and sighing as her father walked away.

Left all alone, Patience found herself watching the large open yard on the other side of the street. After a moment she spotted movement in the barn at the end of the yard, and she realized that several horses had been left stabled in there. She watched the horses for a moment, and then – realizing that nobody else seemed to be about – she made her way into the yard and headed to the barn.

She had always felt a fondness for horses, but she'd always worried about their tough lives in the streets of London. These horses, on the other hand, seemed to be much happier in their stables.

"Hello, there," she said as she stopped at the entrance to the stable and saw a lovely light brown horse standing just a few feet away. "You're beautiful, aren't you? What's your name?"

The horse whinnied briefly, almost as if it was trying to answer, and then – hearing footsteps – Patience turned just in time to see a young man making his way through with a set of leathers in his arms. And then, as the man stopped and stared at her, Patience realized that she'd seen him before.

"You!" she gasped, raising a hand and pointing directly at his face. "You were at the window last night!"

***

"How many times do I have to explain?" Daniel Purkiss said as he set some more leathers on the bench in the yard. "I wasn't sneaking around! I was just looking at the house!"

"You're a very bad liar," she told him, watching from the shade just inside the open doorway. "I saw you. What possible excuse could anyone have for being at my family's home in the middle of the night?"

"I had no idea you'd moved in," he replied. "That house has been empty for longer than I've been alive, and I suppose I just didn't hear anyone mention that there was to be a change."

"So you like to go and poke around outside empty houses, do you?"

"It's not as simple as that."

"My father will be along presently," she replied, "and I shall have to inform him that I've found the miscreant who caused me to scream in the night. And by then, you should probably try to have come up with a much better explanation for your actions."

"You won't like it if I tell you the truth."

"And why's that?"

"Because I was looking for -"

He stopped himself just in time, as if he was worried about her possible response, and then he headed back outside. This time, Patience followed him, and they walked together across the sunny yard until Daniel picked up some more leathers. Patience immediately did the same.

"Be careful," he told her.

"Why?"

"They're heavy."

"I'm not a weakling."

"No, but you're a -"

Again, he stopped himself just in time.

"You're a *lady*," he said diplomatically.

"Then why were you staring in at me last night?"

"I wasn't staring at you," he explained as they both carried some leathers toward the barn. "Not you specifically, at least. I was just trying to see if there was... anything else in there."

"Like what?"

"Do you know the stories about Hadlow House?"

They set the leathers down. Patience's arms were aching, but she refused to show any weakness whatsoever so she immediately followed him back out.

"I know nothing about the house, really," she admitted. "I assume someone must have lived there before us."

"A long time ago."

"Thirty years, my father claims."

"That's about right," he said, stopping and turning to her. He was conspicuously rubbing his arms as if he too was tired. "A little more, perhaps," he added. "The house is fairly new, it was built by the previous occupant. His name was Richard or Robert Hadlow, I forget which exactly. Anyway, you won't get many people willing to utter that name around here, not on account of what he did."

"What did he do?" Patience asked.

"He murdered his wife and servants."

"Are you sure?"

"He shot his wife," Daniel continued. "Shot her in the head, apparently. He also killed his two servants, an elderly couple, and then in a final act of desperation he turned the gun upon himself. From what I heard, the bodies lay undiscovered for some time before anyone even went up there. The Hadlows weren't exactly popular, on account of half of them being Catholics and fighting for the old king."

"So people died in the house?" Patience asked cautiously.

"Three, by my count," he told her, "and then Hadlow himself just outside. And ever since then, until you arrived, the place has stood empty." He paused. "Well, unoccupied, but not necessarily *empty*. In fact, that's why I've been going out there occasionally."

"To look at an empty house?"

"You need to consider the difference between a house being empty and being unoccupied," he told her. "Over the years, people have been talking about Hadlow House. There are certain stories going around, and claims about the place." He paused again, watching her carefully as if he was keen to judge her reaction. "There are plenty of people in Cobblefield," he added finally, "who'll swear to you that the house is haunted."

"By a ghost?"

"People have heard screams," he continued.

"Almost no-one dares to go near the place, but even people going past on the main road into Cobblefield have heard a woman's scream ringing out from the house. If you ask me, that's almost certainly the ghost of Richard Hadlow's wife. After her husband killed her, she was probably left searching for revenge."

"Is that why you were out there last night?" she asked. "Were you looking for a ghost?"

"I've been trying to see her for myself," he explained. "I've never done anything wrong, maybe apart from trespassing on land where I shouldn't be. But I've never tried to get into the house. To be honest, I'm not sure that I'd dare."

"There's no ghost in Hadlow House," she told him, even as she thought back to the touch of that hand on her throat. "Do people actually believe in ghosts out here in the countryside?"

"Where are you from?"

"London, and let me tell you, people in London don't believe in all this talk about ghosts." She took a deep breath, hoping to seem a little more confident. "I suppose it's only natural that you believe in them out here, though," she added. "After all, people in a place like Cobblefield are probably much more simple-minded than Londoners."

"Is that right?" Daniel replied, clearly slightly amused by her suggestion. "Do you think *I'm* simple-minded?"

"Its not your fault," she told him. "Growing up in the countryside, you don't have any real chances to become sophisticated."

"You have soot on your ear," he pointed out.

"You're a stable boy," she countered, as she tried to wipe the soot away, only to stop as she realized that she had no real chance of success. "I bet you've never even been to a big city."

Hearing footsteps, she turned just in time to see her father making his way into the yard. She immediately flinched, worried that she'd get into trouble for talking to one of the local boys, but instead her father seemed a little amused as he stopped and put his hands on his hips.

"Wonderful," he beamed, smiling at Patience for a moment before turning to Daniel. "Boy, tell me, where can I find someone who might sell me one of these horses?"

CHAPTER SEVEN

"YOU SEEM TO BE a natural," Samuel said a couple of hours later, as he made his way on foot toward the large gate at the front of Hadlow House. "We'll make a rider of you yet."

"I rode once or twice in London," Patience reminded him, struggling to stay on the saddle as the horse paced along beneath her. "It's all about -"

Before she could finish, the horse stopped suddenly and she almost fell forward. Grasping the reins, she managed to stay in place, and after a moment she leaned down and patted the horse's flank.

"It's all about staying calm," she continued, although she couldn't entirely chase away the sense of fear in her voice. "He's a big boy, but Daniel swears that he's already well-behaved."

"Did you talk to that Daniel boy for long before I chanced upon you?"

"Only a few seconds," she replied abruptly. "I don't really know what I'd have talked to him about, he's just a country boy with no real experience of the world. Not like me."

"Of course," Samuel said with a faint smile. "I'm going to have to find somewhere to tie this fine fellow up until I can work out a more permanent arrangement. I must confess, I did not plan to actually complete the purchase so quickly, but I shall be able to put the horse to good use."

"Can we name him?" she asked.

"If you wish to."

"How about..."

She paused, trying to think of a suitable name for such a large, fine animal.

"How about Henry?" she suggested finally. "That sounds friendly, doesn't it?"

"Henry," Samuel replied, stepping closer and patting the horse's side. "I suppose I can live with that. He's going to have to learn to work hard, though. I shall need to get about, so there will be much riding and -"

Suddenly the horse lurched back, letting out a loud whinny and rearing up on his hind legs. Patience, too shocked to really know how to react, leaned down and clung to him tight while dropping the reins, but those seemed to only spook Henry further; turning, he seemed ready to gallop away, only for Samuel to race around and grab the reins, holding him steady as the moment of panic seemed to pass.

"What happened?" Patience gasped. "I almost fell right off him!"

"Something troubled him," Samuel replied, stroking the side of the horse's face in an attempt to calm him down a little more. "I want you to climb off now, Patience. Remember that these are working animals, and they should be treated as such. Henry is not your friend."

He paused, before looking up at his daughter.

"Well?" he continued. "Did you hear what I just said, Patience? You must dismount."

***

"I can't believe how people can live in such a small village," Patience said as she stood at the kitchen window, looking out at the horse as it stood tied to a post in the garden. "They must have no idea of how the real world works."

"Are you starting to miss London?" Rose asked, busying herself with some pots on the counter.

"I didn't say that," Patience replied, turning to her, "it's just that I wish there could be some degree of compromise." She paused for a moment, watching as her mother worked. "Do you believe me?" she asked cautiously. "About what happened in the chimney, I mean. I spoke to a boy in town today and he was clearly simple-minded, but he talked about the people who used to live here. Did you know that a man shot his wife and servants dead?"

"Your father mentioned something about that."

"Do you think it's possible that..."

Patience's voice trailed off for a moment as she realized that she risked sounding very foolish.

"Could they still be here in some way?" she asked finally.

"I imagine they were all buried in the cemetery in the village."

"Yes, but I'm not talking about their physical remains." Patience thought for a moment. "I suppose I never much gave the idea a lot of thought back in London, but out here there seems to be more space for such things. Do think it's possible, especially in the wake of some terrible tragedy, for the dead to... stay?"

"No," Rose said firmly, "I most certainly do not."

"So they just go away forever?"

"Their souls are judged," Rose told her, "and then they pass on to whatever place is deemed appropriate. But this should not be news to you, you should know all of this by now."

"I know," Patience continued, "but I keep thinking back to that hand that gripped my -"

"There was no hand," Rose said firmly. "Patience, please, let us not have the same discussion over and over again. You were in an unfamiliar house, in an unfamiliar chimney, and you became disorientated. We shall likely never know exactly what attacked you, but I am absolutely sure that it was one of the Lord's creatures. And by that, I mean a bird or a mouse or... a badger!"

"I would like to think that you're right," Patience murmured softly.

"Soon there will be so much work to do here," Rose replied, "that you will have scant time for such fantasies. You have a keen mind, Patience, and it would be good to keep that mind occupied, lest it might run off on some tangent." They both heard footsteps entering the house, clomping heavily across the hallway and approaching the kitchen. "I shall ask your father to hasten and find more tasks for you."

"The horse was frightened when he saw the house," Patience replied as Samuel entered the room. "That cannot have been for nothing."

"Indeed, it was not," Samuel said, stopping and holding a hand out toward her, displaying his palm. "Fortunately, I believe I have found the culprits."

Stepping closer, Patience looked down and spotted several crumpled black specks on his skin.

"Ants," he continued. "Not any ants I have encountered before, either. These ants bite, and I confess I killed them swiftly before they had a chance to do so again. We appear to have a nest of ants somewhere on the property, and they had already found their way onto the horse's hooves. What happened next should be clear to anyone, they bit him as well, causing him to recoil. When I examined the ground, I found many more of them. They are unusually aggressive, so I shall make sure to locate their nest immediately so that I can destroy them all. Until then, keep an eye out for them whenever you are working in the garden."

"Ants?" Patience replied, peering even more closely at the crushed corpses on her father's hand. "Could ants frighten a horse so much?"

"A few of them bit *me*," Samuel told her. "The sensation is not pleasant."

"Boiling water will get rid of them," Rose said, taking one of the larger pots and hauling it onto the counter. "Samuel, there's no time like the present when it comes to pests. I shall boil some water up, and then I'll bring it out to you when you've located the nest. That way, with any luck, we can have these wretched things gone by the evening.

“That is for the best,” he replied.

“Horrible things,” Rose added, looking at the ants for a moment before lifting the pot again and carrying it toward the back door. “I won't tolerate them coming into the house, that's for sure.”

“I have some provisions arriving shortly,” Samuel told her. “Until that moment, I shall search for the nest. The task shouldn't take long, I must merely follow the line of these wretches until I discover some hold in the ground.”

“And I shall have the water ready,” Rose told him. “Or, rather, Patience and I shall do the work.” She turned to her daughter. “I believe young minds should be kept busy, so that they do not latch onto troublesome matters that might later cause bother.”

“I'm not a little girl,” Patience told her.

“I don't mind who prepares the water,” Samuel said as he brushed the dead ants from his hands and turned to go to the door, “only that it gets done. The sooner we get rid of these troublesome little things, the better.”

“Do you really think that mere ants could disturb a horse so greatly?” Patience asked her mother, as Samuel left the room. “Henry is such a big animal, and those ants are tiny. Surely any horse would merely laugh at the ants and continue on its way, rather than allowing itself to become so terribly spooked.”

“Small creatures can be of great annoyance to big creatures,” Rose pointed out, “especially if they learn where best to bite. Now get out into the garden and find a spot where we can build a small fire. I have a feeling that your father won't rest until these ants have been dealt with once and for all.”

CHAPTER EIGHT

AS FLAMES CONTINUED TO crackle and burn beneath the large metal pot, Patience reached forward and warmed her hands. Although the afternoon was by no means cold, she still enjoyed the sensation of a little extra heat on her skin, and she found the sight of the fire to be somewhat mesmerizing.

"I shall go and see how your father is getting along," Rose muttered, traipsing past the fire. "In his pursuit of those ants, he seems to have gone all the way around to the rear of the house. I hope there's not a big infestation, otherwise our work here will sure never be done."

She sighed.

"You know what your father is like," she added. "He can become terribly fixated on the smaller jobs, for want of taking in the bigger picture."

Left alone, Patience continued her meditation, watching the flames and trying to find some joy in the simpler things. That was something her mother had urged her to do several times: take comfort in the simple pleasures in life, especially out in the countryside, and try to forget about the complicated world of London. In truth, Patience felt torn between the two worlds, and she couldn't help but feel as if the silence of the countryside masked some hidden danger. Still, she quickly reminded herself that her life had changed now, and that she had to find joy wherever she could.

She had to learn to like simple things.

Hearing a rustling sound, she turned just in time to see a figure approaching the property on horseback. She squinted a little, trying to get a better look; the figure had some bags with him, and after a moment Patience remembered that her father had arranged for some provisions to be delivered from the village. And then, as the horse stopped and the rider dismounted, Patience realized that she recognized this particular individual.

A faint smile immediately reached her lips.

***

"And how does the great Hadlow House appear to

you in the daytime?" she asked as she led Daniel toward the front door. "Is it more or less fearsome than at night?"

"In truth, it appears to be just another house," he replied, struggling a little with the bags as he followed her across the garden. "In fact, it's more beautiful than I anticipated."

"My father has plans to make it even more so."

"I've heard a lot about this house," he continued. "According to people in the village, Mr. Hadlow intended to turn this into the most wonderful property in the entire county. He was trying to distance himself from family troubles from the past and he had the money to commission a number of great plans. By all accounts, however, he didn't live long enough to see those plans come to fruition."

"Much of his furniture was left behind," she told him. "As far as I can tell, the quality was very good indeed. Certainly better than one might expect for this part of the world."

Pushing the door open, she began to make her way across the hallway. After a moment, however, she realized that she had not heard the sound of Daniel joining her. She stopped and turned, and to her great amusement she saw that he seemed almost fearful as he stopped in the doorway, silhouetted against the garden beyond.

"Well?" she said. "Is something the matter?"

"No," he replied, but his voice betrayed the truth, "it's just that..."

"What?"

She waited, and after a moment she began to realize why he was holding back. As her eyes adjusted to being in the hallway, and as she was better able to make out his face, she saw genuine fear in his eyes.

"You've never actually been inside the house, have you?" she said. "For all your talk of its history and its supposed ghosts, you've only ever seen it from the outside."

"I told you, I never forced my way in. I'm not a trespasser."

"Does it look so awful?" she asked, holding her arms up as if to demonstrate that there was no danger. "Do you see some awful spirit looming from the shadows?"

He hesitated.

"No," he admitted after a moment.

"And do you sense some great evil?"

"No."

"And do you hear any groans coming from the dead, or perhaps the banging of chains?"

"No."

"So I think it's safe," she continued, although she could tell now that his fear was absolutely genuine, and she found this to be a somewhat endearing quality. "There really is nothing here that is going to cause you harm. Well, not unless you fear *me*, that is."

A few seconds later, as if the effort required was great, Daniel stepped into the house. He looked around, as if he still expected to spot some awful creature rushing at him from any direction.

"It's big," he admitted. "Bigger than it looks from the outside, almost. I've never been inside such a big house."

"It's also rundown," she said, gesturing for him to follow as she turned and led him into the kitchen. "My father might not like me being alone in the house with a boy I don't know, but I'm sure it'll be alright as long as we don't get too close." Her footsteps rang loud against the bare boards as she walked across the kitchen. "I'm curious, though. Most of the houses in Cobblefield looked quite small, almost like cottages." She turned to him again. "Is this the biggest house in the area?"

She waited for an answer, but Daniel had stopped again, looking around the kitchen with a fresh expression of fear on his face.

"Is this where it happened?" he asked.

"Is this where *what* happened?"

"Is this where Mr. Hadlow murdered his wife and servants?"

"I have absolutely no idea," she told him.

"Do you know what I heard?" He hurried

over to her and placed the bags on the counter between them. “I heard something even more shocking and unusual. According to a doctor whose father attended the scene at the time, Mr. Hadlow had sawn off the arm of one of his servants.”

Patience raised a skeptical eyebrow.

“A doctor wouldn't lie!” he added.

“This tale becomes stranger with each telling,” she pointed out. “Next time you talk about the history of the house, no doubt you shall throw in some flying dragons for good measure.”

“I'm being serious!”

“So am I!”

She opened her mouth to tell him once again that she was not falling for his stories, but at that moment she spotted movement outside. Looking out the window, she saw that her parents were at the very farthest end of the rear garden, and that they seemed to be utterly focused on the task of searching for the ants' nest. At that moment, realizing that she might not get another chance to speak her mind, she turned to Daniel and found herself wondering whether she could trust him entirely. He seemed like a decent, perhaps slightly simple fellow, and she felt sure that she had the measure of him in case he tried anything untoward. After all, in London she'd had to protect herself once or twice from badly-behaved boys in the streets, and she was sure that country boys would be even easier to handle.

"There has been one thing," she said cautiously.

He tilted his head slightly, like a dog.

"I am telling you this because nobody else believes me," she added. "My parents certainly seem to think me a liar or a fool, but I swear that this happened. I should not care about what other people believe or don't believe, yet it irks me to find that no-one else accepts even the slightest possibility."

"What?" he asked.

Again she opened her mouth to reply, and again she held back. She hated the idea of showing any weakness or even uncertainty, yet in that moment she felt that she might finally have found someone who would listen to her concerns. She looked out the window once more, just to check that her parents were still busy chasing ants, and then she turned to Daniel again before stepping around from behind the counter.

"There is one thing that happened," she said, lowering her voice a little, "and in truth I cannot stop thinking about it."

She turned her head slightly, so that he could better see the side of her neck.

"Do you notice some marks?"

"I do."

Thinking back to the touch of that dead

hand, she felt a shiver pass through her body.

"What caused them?" Daniel asked cautiously.

"Something attacked me," she admitted. "I was upstairs. Well, in a way. It's a little difficult to explain. I think, instead, I had better show you."

CHAPTER NINE

"SO... YOU WERE *IN* the wall?"

"I was in the chimney," Patience replied, "and there is this hole, as you can see. And then a hand came through, and this hand most certainly did not belong to either my mother or my father. It grabbed me, here."

She reached up and placed one of her own hands around her throat.

"I believe it meant to cause me even greater harm than it managed."

"It gave you those scratches?"

"And it was cold," she told him. "As cold as ice, or as cold as..."

She paused, wondering whether to admit that the hand had felt dead. Not that she knew what a dead hand felt like, of course, but she certainly had her suspicions.

"Then there was someone in this room," he said, stepping forward and then reaching into the gap, pushing his hand through into the chimney. "There was someone in this bedroom, and they had cause – or so they believed – to attack you."

"Do you believe me?"

"I see no reason not to," he replied.

She felt a rush of relief. Finally, after so very long, she was no longer being subjected to doubt and derision. For a moment she wanted to rush forward and embrace him in a hug, although she quickly reminded herself that such an action would be wildly inappropriate and might cause great damage to her own reputation. Either that, or he might misunderstand her actions, in which case she would have to fight him off.

"So someone was standing where I am," he continued, "and they reached through here, and evidently they meant to do you harm. Grave harm, from what you've told me."

Worried that she might be discovered by her parents, and that they might not be entirely happy to find her alone in a bedroom with a strange boy, Patience hurried to the window and looked out. To her relief, she saw that her father was all the way over by the old oak tree, still inspecting the ground; her mother, meanwhile, had returned to the fire and was busy sorting through wood to use as she worked to get the pot of water boiling. They both seemed entirely focused on their work, and Patience breathed a sigh of relief as she turned to Daniel again.

"There are two candidates, as far as I see it," he told her as he pulled his arm out from the hole. "There is the wife of Mr. Hadlow, or there is his servant. Either one of them must still be in the house somehow."

"But they're dead," she pointed out.

"And your neck is cut," he replied. "At some point, we must acknowledge the facts that are before us. There's clearly something in this house that you don't understand, that none of us can comprehend, and it attacked you. How can you be sure that something similar won't happen again?"

"My father is going to seal that hole in the bricks."

"There will be other opportunities."

She hesitated, before looking out the window again. Her father was still examining the ground near the oak tree, and her mother was now boiling some water.

"Screams are heard sometimes," Daniel continued.

She turned to him.

"From the road," he added. "Most nights, in fact. I know you haven't been here for very long, but have you heard -"

"Nothing," she said, interrupting him. "No screams, certainly."

"People say that the scream usually comes at around three in the morning," he told her. "I have not heard it myself, but I would be willing. Do you think you might be awake at such a time? Do you think perhaps you would consider coming to the road and meeting me? I promise you'll be safe."

"I cannot go out at three o'clock in the morning," she told him. "The idea is utterly ludicrous."

"But -"

"I should never have told you any of this," she replied, glancing out the window again. She saw her mother kneeling to work next to the boiling pot, and then she turned to Daniel again. Before she could get another word out, however, she realized that something was wrong.

Had she not, in that split second glance, seen a second woman standing just next to her mother?

Suddenly a cry rang out, and she turned to see that the pot of water had spilled over. Rose was screaming and scrambling back as the boiling water spread out across the muddy ground.

***

"What happened?" Patience gasped as soon as she ran out from the front of the house. "Mother, are you alright?"

"Your mother is burned," Samuel said, helping Rose up while holding a cloth around her hands. "Boiling water. We must get her inside."

"But what happened?" Patience asked.

"Fetch some fresh water from the river," he said firmly as he led the trembling, sobbing Rose past Daniel and into the house. "It must be cold. Hurry!"

Looking down, Patience saw that steam was rising from the boiling water that had soaked the ground. The large metal pot, meanwhile, lay overturned nearby, as if some force had toppled it from its position on the fire. The flames were still burning, and after a moment Patience looked all around as she remembered the strange woman she'd glimpsed so briefly.

"Water!" Daniel said, grabbing the pot and hurrying toward the river. "Every second counts!"

"Who are you?" Patience asked, trembling with fear as she looked all around. There was no sign of the other woman, but her gray dress had seemed strangely familiar.

"Hurry!" Samuel shouted from inside the house, as Rose cried out again. "For the love of God, Patience, we need cold water!"

Spurred into action, Patience hurried around the fire and made her way toward the river. Ahead, she could see Daniel already clambering down the muddy bank, while the two horses – which remained tied up near the gate – seemed increasingly agitated. By the time she reached the edge of the river and looked down, Patience saw that Daniel had already collected a fair amount, and he was scrambling back up the bank to meet her.

"How bad are the burns?" he asked breathlessly.

"I don't know," she replied, before grabbing the pot from him. "I must go to her. You should leave."

"But -"

"Just go!" she hissed, taking a step back. "I should never have told you about such things. If I hadn't, perhaps that woman would not have appeared again just now."

"What are you talking about?"

"Leave!" she hissed, before turning and almost stumbling as she began to carry the heavy pot of cold water toward the house. "You're slowing me down!"

"Meet me on the road at three in the morning!" he called after her. "If you can, at least! I'll be there!"

Ignoring him, she hurried into the house. She almost tripped on the front step, but she managed to stay upright while also holding onto the pot. Already, she could hear her mother crying in the kitchen, and as she rushed across the hallway she could already tell that Rose was in a great deal of pain. She soon found that her parents had gone out through the back door and were kneeling on the grass, so she followed them and stopped, only to see to her horror that her mother's hands were red raw and covered in burned, peeling skin that left the meat beneath exposed.

"Hurry!" Samuel said, grabbing the pot of water and immediately pouring it over Rose's shaking hands.

Screaming, Rose pulled away, sobbing wildly as she tumbled down against the mud.

"We need more!" Samuel muttered, passing the pot back to Patience before scrambling around behind his wife and hauling her up. "Damn it, Patience, you're no use if you merely stand there with your mouth hanging open like that!"

Getting to his feet, he grabbed the pot and hurried around the house.

"I shall fetch it myself!" he shouted. "You're no use in a panic, Patience! Keep hold of your mother until I return!"

"I'm sorry," Patience stammered, before stepping over to her mother. "It's alright, there's no need to -"

In that moment she froze, as she saw the full extent of Rose's injuries. Both hands were burned to such an extent that Patience scarcely believed what she was seeing; the flesh seemed to have begun to fall away, revealing the thick sinews and tendons beneath, with scraps of curled white skin dangling down and some having fallen onto the grass. Blood was running down onto Rose's wrist, and after a moment the poor woman let out a howl of agony as tears streamed from her eyes.

"Help me!" she gasped, reaching toward Patience with bloodied hands that looked almost to be melting. "Patience, please, this was no accident!"

CHAPTER TEN

AN OWL HOOTED SOMEWHERE in the distance. Flat on her back in bed, Patience stared up at the darkness and tried to ignore the sound of her mother's pained sobbing coming from the next room.

She had no idea how many hours had passed since she'd retired for the night, but Patience could tell that her mother was in far too much pain to sleep. With her badly-injured hands heavily wrapped in fabric, Rose had been told by Samuel that she simply needed to wait until morning to see whether there might be any improvement; Samuel knew that there was a doctor in the village, although he'd heard that this particular doctor traveled regularly and might not be available instantly. He'd promised to go and ask around, but for now Rose was supposed to somehow last the night despite the agony that was still burning in both hands.

Finally, sitting up, Patience looked over at the window and saw that tops of the nearby trees bathed in moonlight. She had no idea of the time, but she couldn't help but think of Daniel possibly sitting out there on the road beyond the forest. Even though she hated the idea of indulging him, she found herself remembering his final words as she'd raced away from him with the pot of water in her hands.

"Meet me on the road at three in the morning! If you can, at least! I'll be there!"

Until this moment, she hadn't seriously considered doing any such thing. Now, however, she was wide awake and she had begun to contemplate the possibility that she might sneak out of the house and go to the road. If nothing else, she wanted to prove to Daniel – and to herself – that her mother's accident had been nothing more than a moment of misfortune, and that the hand in the chimney had been imagined.

Finally, taking care to make as little noise as possible, she began to climb out of bed.

***

As she reached the end of the muddy road and stopped to look around, Patience immediately spotted a figure sitting on the low brick wall opposite. She took a moment to adjust her gown, and to remind herself that this idea was absolute folly, and then she stepped out across the main road and began to approach the figure.

"This is so foolish," she muttered under her breath. "Was I born with no sense at all?"

"You came," Daniel said.

"Only because I happened to be awake," she told him.

"As did I. Lately I find that I sleep in such fits and starts, I never quite know how much rest I shall get. As well as that, my father's clock is broken, so I have no way of telling the exact time."

"How long have you been sitting here for?" she asked.

"A while."

"I have not come unarmed," she added, reaching into her pocket and pulling out the knife she'd brought from the kitchen. "I should warn you that I am not some defenseless maiden."

"I never took you to be one," he replied, before reaching into his own pocket and pulling out an even larger knife. "I too came prepared."

"To attack me?"

"To defend myself." He chuckled. "I don't know what you London girls are like. For all I'm aware, you might have a taste for human flesh."

"You are quite out of your mind," she

replied, stopping next to him and turning to look back toward the house. "Well? I am here. For what purpose have you dragged me out here?"

"How is your mother?"

"She will live," she told him. "As for the state of her hands, I am not sure. One thing is certain, however, and that is that I shall have to take on all of her duties until she is well, and that might be quite some time."

"I'm sorry."

"I can handle it," she said defiantly. "Do not try to change the subject. Are we going to hear some kind of ethereal scream or not?"

"What does that word mean?"

"Ethereal?" She shook her head. "It doesn't matter. What matters is that I'm cold, and my father will be furious if he finds that I have crept out in the middle of the night." She watched the pitch-black trees and thought of Hadlow House waiting somewhere in the darkness; the thought sent another shiver through her bones, and she was immediately reminded of her isolation. "The silence is quite astonishing."

"Do you miss London?"

"The grime? The smog?" She turned to him. "The mass of people?"

"I can imagine that such things might be intoxicating," he suggested. "For some people."

"I merely feel that I have gone from one

extreme to the other," she told him. "From a crush so awful that I feared I might not be able to breathe, to a place so empty that I could scream and nobody would hear."

"It's not so bad here."

"Do you mean to never leave?"

"I have a good job," he replied. "My father is a blacksmith, as his father was a blacksmith was before him, and his father as well."

"And you will be a blacksmith?"

"What else should I do?" he asked. "It's not as if one can simply choose a profession."

"And you will be in need of a wife, I presume."

"Are you volunteering?"

"No!" she blurted out, before turning to once again look at the forest. She knew she was blushing, and that her embarrassment was only saved by the moonlight. "I merely meant that you will have to find someone in the village."

"No doubt I shall."

"No doubt you shall."

They sat in silence for a moment, and a moment later a cry rang out in the distance. Patience immediately got to her feet, but a few seconds later she realized that Daniel was laughing.

"That was a fox," he told her.

"It sounded like a person."

"Foxes do that."

"How do you know?"

"I was born and raised in Cobblefield," he pointed out. "Do you even *have* foxes in London?"

"Not that I am aware of," she replied. "I must say, however, that they seem to make the most frightful sounds. Why exactly would an animal imitate the scream of a woman?"

"There are many reasons," he told her. "To attract a mate. To mark their territory. To warn away predators."

"You seem to know a lot about them."

"I know about the world in which I live," he replied. "To me, that seems only wise. Do you have any idea just how many different creatures live around here? Why, I'm sure that many of them approach your house during the night, and that's only the larger animals. There are insects, too, and all sorts of bugs and other crawling little things."

"I'm not sure I like the sound of that," she replied as another shudder passed through her body. "In London we have only to deal with dirt. And other people."

"Then I understand why Cobblefield and its surroundings must come as such a shock," he continued. "You really are a fish out of water, Ms. Butler, are you not? And while you will certainly adjust to your new life, I find myself wondering whether you will ever truly settle. There seems to be something of the city ingrained in your bones."

"Now you're just speaking of things you know nothing about," she told him, before pausing for a moment. "I am struck," she added, "by the sense that you and I are almost from two entirely different worlds."

"We're still people, at the end of the day," he suggested. "I'm still a boy, you're still a girl, and we seem to still have the same broad understanding of the world around us. Indeed, you have a sense of curiosity that I quite admire." Now it was his turn to pause, watching her eyes for a little longer than she felt was appropriate. "I have always found intelligence to be a most admirable trait in a woman," he told her, "and you seem to have intelligence in abundance. Indeed, there is a fire in your eyes that I have never seen before."

"If there is fire in my eyes," she replied, "then that would seem to indicate a quite catastrophic turn of events."

She waited for him to smile, or even to laugh, but she quickly realized that he was merely staring. She felt a little uncomfortable, although she did not necessarily want to turn away; instead, she met his stare and waited to see what he would do next, and after just a moment he began to move his face a little closer.

Suddenly a scream rang out, rising high above the darkened forest, and Patience immediately turned to look back toward the house.

"That was no fox!" Daniel said, getting to his feet. "That came from Hadlow House!"

CHAPTER ELEVEN

RACING ALONG THE DARK path that led to the house, Patience almost tripped as she spotted the large gate up ahead. Henry was still tied to a post nearby, but as Patience reached the gate she saw that there were no lights burning inside the house.

"Wait for me!" Daniel shouted breathlessly.

Pulling the gate open, Patience hurried along the path that led across the garden. Her heart was racing and she knew that something must be terribly wrong, but as she reached the front door and pushed it open she found once again that the house was bathed in darkness. She made her way up the stairs, taking no care this time to avoid making a sound, and finally she burst into her parents' room and saw two shapes sleeping beneath the covers.

After a moment, one of those shapes began

to stir, followed by the other.

"Who is that?" Samuel barked. "Identify yourself!"

"Patience?" Rose whimpered, sitting up. "What are you doing?"

"Are you both alright?" Patience asked, as she heard Daniel racing up the stairs behind her.

"We were sleeping," Samuel told her. "You should be as well and -"

He suddenly jumped out of his bed and hurried across the room, racing past Patience and pushing Daniel back.

"Who are you?" he shouted. "Are you the boy from the yard? Why are you in my home?"

"That's Daniel!" Patience gasped, pulling her father away. "He's my friend!"

"I am?" Daniel replied, clearly shocked.

"You do not have any friends here!" Samuel said firmly, turning to her. "If you did, they would not be young men! And they were, you most certainly would not be consorting with them in the middle of the night!"

"I was not consorting with anyone," she replied through gritted teeth. "Father, I merely went to meet Daniel on the road. I know how that sounds, but I can explain later. Once I was out there, we both heard the scream and came racing back."

"What scream?" Samuel asked.

"It was the most awful scream," she told

him. "It sounded like a woman." She turned to look at her mother. In the darkness, she could just about see her sitting up still on the bed. "Mother, did something happen to you?"

"Your mother did not scream," Samuel said firmly. "I might have been asleep, but I would most assuredly have heard such a thing."

"I was not asleep," Ruth said, her voice tense with pain. "I wish I had been, but the pain in my hands has made sleep impossible all through this night."

"Then you heard the scream?" Patience asked.

"I heard a fox, a short while ago."

"This scream was nothing like that of a fox," Patience told her impatiently. "A fox *did* call out, you are correct, but then a short while later a woman screamed. Nobody within three miles could have missed such an awful sound. Father, if it did not stir you from sleep, that is a surprise but it is at least understandable. Mother, if you were awake, you could not possibly have not heard this sound."

"I have heard creaks and groans from the house all night," Ruth told her. "I even believe now that I heard you sneaking out, although at the time I believed this was just the sound of the house settling. However, as the Lord is my witness, I heard no scream."

"Tell them!" Patience said, turning to

Daniel. "Tell them that we both heard it!"

"Your daughter speaks the truth," Daniel said, although he sounded more than a little nervous. "Mr. Butler, I would not lie. A cry rang out, a most dreadful sound, and it seemed to come from here. From this very house."

"You must have heard it!" Patience said firmly. "Father! Mother! You must have heard this scream!"

***

"So what am I to do?" Samuel asked a short while later as he stood in the kitchen, watching Patience sitting at the table. "My daughter goes running around in the middle of the night with some boy from the village, and then she imagines strange sounds. Tell me, what is a man supposed to do in my position?"

"You could try believing me," she told him. " Daniel heard it too!"

"This Daniel boy is halfway home by now," he reminded her, "and mark my words, I *shall* speak to his father about everything that has happened tonight. But in truth, his conduct is none of my concern, other than that he stays well away from you." He sighed. "Patience, your mother and I have always striven to raise you well. In London you were a serious-minded young lady who never spoke of anything unusual, yet here in the countryside some great change seems to have come over you."

"I am only telling you what I heard," she replied. "And, earlier, what I saw."

"You are not adjusting well to this change," he muttered. "Not well at all. I was told once that children, especially daughters, can sometimes cause trouble as they grow up. I had naively believed, Patience, that you were cut from a different cloth, but now I realize that I was wrong."

He paused, before stepping toward her.

"Your mother is ill," he continued, and now there was a hint of pleading in his voice. "You have seen her hands. She is in terrible pain and will remain that way for quite some time. I need you to take on many, if not all, of her responsibilities around the house. I myself am going to be very busy over the next few days, familiarizing myself with the area and the land and the various properties that I must supervise on behalf of Mr. Wallace. I cannot afford to let him down. Do you understand that?"

"Yes, but -"

"Do you understand, Patience?" he asked again, much more firmly this time.

"Yes!" she hissed angrily, "but -"

"Then that is the end of the discussion," he told her, cutting her off again. "Learn from your mother. You must not only perform her duties in the house, you must do so while holding your tongue whenever you are irritated or annoyed. Your mother works so hard to make sure that I have a good home to which I can return after I have worked, and that is very important to me. Your mother and I are a team, and until she is better, you are going to have to take her place. This is not a bad thing, Patience. You will learn so much and grow up faster."

"We are not alone in this house," she whispered.

"What did you just say?"

"Nothing," she replied. "Nothing at all. Why would I? If I am never to be believed, then why would I bother to say a single word? I might as well be mute."

"The sun will rise soon," he pointed out. "There is no use returning to bed, we might as well both stay up and let your mother rest for a while. I shall prepare the horse and leave a little early, and your mother should be well enough to guide you through your duties for the day." He paused, watching her with a growing sense of concern. "Patience," he added, "I hope I do not need to say this, but I'm sure you understand that under no circumstances are you ever to see that Daniel Purkiss boy again. Is that understood?"

"He did nothing wrong!" she protested.

"I don't care," he said firmly. "There is to be no fraternization between you and anyone from the village. Not without my say-so. You're growing up to become a charming young lady, Patience, and the time will soon come when I must entertain possible suitors for your hand in marriage. Until then, you are most certainly not going to examine the possible candidates for yourself. Is that clear?"

"Yes, Father," she said bitterly, for she knew that she had no choice.

"I shall be away once the sun comes up," he continued, "and you shall have a range of chores to complete. You might find these chores burdensome, but you will soon come to appreciate the value of having your mind occupied by honest work. It is idle minds, Patience, that dream up fantasies about strange screams in the night and... hands suddenly appearing in chimneys."

"Yes, Father," she said again, and somehow she sounded even more bitter than before. "Whatever you say, Father."

As Samuel left the room, Patience was left sitting alone at the large, long table. She looked out at the garden, and she could see the very first rays of morning light starting to brighten the sky behind the trees. Dawn was coming, and for Patience this meant that a very long day of work was shortly to begin.

CHAPTER TWELVE

"THIS WILL BE FINE," Father Ward said as he examined the metalwork on the church door. "Tell your father that, as usual, he has done us all proud."

"I'll let him know," Daniel replied as he gathered his tools. "Of course, there will be no charge, not for you. My father always says that any service we provide to the church should be thought of as a service provided to God."

"Your father is very kind," Father Ward told him. "And do you think that you will follow in his footsteps and take over the business? I hear that your father's back is getting worse and that some days he is barely able to get out of bed. I'm sure that you and your sister help as best you can, but there must come a moment in every man's life when he has to accept his own limitations."

"He gets by," Daniel explained, "but I'm learning more and more every day. He directs me well, and I dare say that eventually I shall have to take charge." He paused for a moment, before glancing across the sunlit cemetery. "Father Ward," he continued cautiously, "how long have you been here at St. Leonard's?"

"Almost all my life," Father Ward replied. "That's coming up on fifty years now."

"Did you ever meet a man named Richard Hadlow?"

At the merest mention of that name, Father Ward visibly stiffened.

"He built a house just beyond the edge of the village," Daniel continued.

"I know that," Father Ward replied. "I remember Richard Hadlow well, he was indeed a generous man. At least, that is how it seemed to me, until..."

His voice trailed off.

"Until what?" Daniel asked. "I know that he killed his wife and his servants."

"It's a little more complicated than that."

"How so?"

"One of his servants died in some kind of accident on the grounds of the house," Father Ward explained. "Baxter, the man's name was. Richard Hadlow went to the great trouble of having him buried here in the cemetery. Then, a short time later, he made the same arrangements for his first wife, and for another servant as well."

"Did he not kill them?"

"You should not listen to rumors."

"I thought the story was that he murdered them all," Daniel replied.

"The Baxters are resting in the cemetery just around that corner behind you," Father Ward told him, "along with the body of Mr. Hadlow's first wife Catherine. Then, not long after they were interred, Mr. Hadlow and his second wife were indeed found dead out at the house."

"Did Mr. Hadlow kill her before ending his own life?"

"That is how the common version of the story goes."

"Don't you believe it?"

"I consider myself to be a good judge of character," Father Ward told him cautiously, as if he was choosing his words with great care, "and although I know that such matters are never absolute, I believe that I knew Richard Hadlow well enough to consider him a good man. The idea that he would have turned his pistol upon his wife Rebecca, and then upon himself, has never quite sat easy with me. Most people around here were very quick to rush to judgment, they'd written Hadlow off as a murderer before he was even in his grave."

"What do *you* think happened?"

"I don't think it's my place to question such things. But why do you ask? Most people around these parts prefer to keep the name Hadlow from their lips."

"Some people have moved into the house."

"So I have heard. Indeed, I expect a visit from the gentleman in question at some point. He has taken on the supervision of much land around these parts, and I'm quite sure that he'll want to know my view on a few matters." He paused for a moment. "My advice, young Mr. Purkiss, would be for you to not bother yourself too much with events of the past. Your have your father to help, and your sister Anne too. As for the Hadlows, they are long gone and buried."

"Do you believe in ghosts, Father Ward?" Daniel asked.

"I do not," the priest said firmly. "Not in the manner you're thinking of, at least. Now go and tell your father that the job here is done. And thank him for his generosity."

***

A few minutes later, having slipped around to the rear of the cemetery, Daniel knelt on the grass and looked at one of the gravestones. His mother Mary had died a little over fifteen years previously, while giving birth to his sister Anne, and Daniel made a point of often visiting the grave so that he could lay a few wild flowers.

Having been only six years old when his mother died, Daniel remembered her very little.

"Father isn't well," he said, even though he knew most likely she couldn't hear him. "He tries to hide the pain in his back, but I see the proof every day in his eyes. I don't know how much longer he can go on like this, but so far he resists any talk of the future. He teaches me how to take on his role, yet I'm really not sure that I'm ready to deal with the family trade. I wish..."

His voice trailed off for a few seconds.

"I wish that you were around to offer me some advice," he continued finally. "I can't help but feel that your role, if you had lived, would have been to help in a situation such as this."

Taking a deep breath, he reminded himself yet again that talking to a grave was foolish. He thought about the coffin deep beneath the ground, and he imagined his mother's body resting down there; he'd heard descriptions of her, of course, but he couldn't help wondering how she looked now, after so long in the darkness. Was there any flesh left on her at all, or had the worms burrowed their way through and had their fill?

"Why do I think such dark thoughts?" he muttered. "I don't even know why I come here, except that I know nobody else does. If I were to stay away, your grave would be entirely forgotten, and that does not seem right to me. Still, there's no good to be had from this melancholy."

Getting to his feet, he took a moment to brush grass from his knees.

"I shall be back," he told his mother. "I promise."

Turning, he began to make his way toward the gate, only to stop as he spotted one particular name on a nearby headstone. Making his way over, he saw that this stone actually bore two separate names.

"Oliver Baxter," he whispered, reading from the stone, "and Frances Baxter."

Realizing that these were the two servants whose deaths had been ascribed to the actions of Richard Hadlow, Daniel reached out and touched the top of the stone. He knew that he was being foolish, of course, yet he couldn't help but feel that he had some connection now to the events at Hadlow House, and he found himself wondering what the Baxters would say now if they were able to talk.

A little further off, another headstone revealed two more names that caught Daniel's attention.

"Richard Hadlow," he read out loud. "Rebecca Hadlow."

Next to that stone, there stood another.

"Catherine Hadlow," he said softly.

He thought for a moment about these lost lives, of which he knew only a few scraps of detail. They had all been dead for more than thirty years. Indeed, they would have already been in their graves by the time Daniel was born, and he realized that it was almost impossible for him to comprehend the lives of people who had lived so long ago. At the same time, he remembered the scream he'd heard during the previous night, and he wondered whether that scream had come from the ghostly lips of Catherine or Rebecca Hadlow, or perhaps from Frances Baxter. The thought sent a sudden chill through his bones.

"I hope you're all resting in peace," he said quietly, supposing that he should show as much respect to the dead as possible. "Whatever happened out there at that house, I hope now you're far away from it all, and that you're not still tormented by the manner of your deaths."

He paused, and after a few seconds he felt a sense of peace wash through his body. As he stared at the various graves, he realized that there was no way their occupants could feel anything other than total contentment. Their earthly struggles were over, and any suggestion that their spirits might linger seemed – in that moment – entirely foolish.

CHAPTER THIRTEEN

"ARE YOU PEELING THOSE carrots properly?" Rose asked sternly. "Tell me the truth, Patience!"

"I'm doing exactly as you instructed," Patience replied, trying to live up to her name as she continued to peel the skins from the carrots. "You don't need to worry, I'm perfectly capable of doing all this."

"That's what you think, but you're too young to know much. I'm sure you're making all sorts of mistakes."

Sighing, Patience glanced over her shoulder and saw her mother still sitting at the table. Ever since Samuel had left on the horse, Rose had been increasingly tetchy, to the extent that she seemed convinced that everyone was trying to undermine her authority. Her hands were wrapped in fabric; for all his talk of seeking medical attention, that morning Samuel had insisted that Rose's hands would recover naturally if only they were left alone. Patience had wondered whether a doctor might yet offer some additional assistance, but Samuel had been certain. Now, however, Rose looked to be in a great deal of pain.

"Mother," Patience said cautiously, "can I help you with your hands?"

"There's nothing to do."

"I know Father was keen to avoid upsetting you, but I keep thinking that -"

"Are you second-guessing your father now?" Rose barked, turning to her. "Is that a little arrogance showing through in your heart?"

"No, of course not," Patience replied, returning her attention to the carrots while wondering whether she could say anything right. Coming to the conclusion that she could not, she resolved to instead speak as little as possible while trying to get on with the tasks at hand. She understood that her mother was in pain, but that didn't make the situation any more bearable. "I was only trying to help."

"Well, you haven't been helping at all," Ruth spat back at her. "Did you bring in that wood from outside?"

"I was going to do it after -"

"There's no point saying you're *going* to do

things," Rose continued. "Do it, or don't do it. Nobody likes hearing a list of excuses."

"I think I'm done with the carrots," Patience said, setting the last of them aside and then heading to the back door. "I'll go and fetch the wood now."

"Have you cleaned up properly?"

"And I'll do that just as soon as I'm back," Patience replied, while reminding herself that she had to remain civil. "Just wait one moment, Mother. I'll have the wood inside and then I'll get on with all the other jobs."

***

As she lifted the first pile of logs, Patience felt a tightening pain in her lower back. She paused for a moment, waiting for the sensation to pass, while telling herself that she was far too young to be suffering from such maladies.

"Mother will be better soon," she muttered under her breath, before turning and looking across the garden. "There's no -"

Before she could finish, she spotted a man standing over by the oak tree. She hesitated, wondering at first whether her father had perhaps returned early from his rounds, but in truth she could already tell that this was someone else; the man in question had his back to her, but he was wearing a rather dirty white shirt and his head was almost entirely bald, save from some gray hair on the sides. Something else seemed different about him, perhaps about the way he was standing, but Patience couldn't quite put her finger on the matter of what she'd noticed.

She opened her mouth to call through to her mother, but at the last second she realized that she needed to prove that she could deal with the situation herself.

After setting the wood down again, and feeling another twinge of pain in her back, she began to make her way across the garden. She tried to remind herself that there was no reason to be afraid, yet something about the man made her feel strangely uneasy. He still looked strange in some way, and as she stopped just a few feet behind him she tried to determine exactly why his shoulders were stooped in such an unusual manner. And then, as she was about to ask him what he wanted, she realized what was wrong.

He only had one arm.

"Hello?" she said cautiously, worried that some stranger from the village had accidentally wandered onto the property. "Can I help you?"

She waited, but the man offered no reply; indeed, he showed no sign that he'd even heard her voice.

"I'm sorry," she continued, "but this is my father's house and I'm not sure that you should be here."

This time, as she waited, she began to wonder how she might defend herself. She knew there was some gardening equipment by the back door, and after a moment she instinctively took a step back as she realized that she might have to run for safety. The man looked old, but she had no confidence that she would be able to outrun him and she could already feel a tightening sense of fear in her chest.

Finally, slowly, the man began to turn to her.

"She's still here," he said, his voice sounding harsh and gravelly.

"I beg your -"

"She's still here," he said again. "She's been here all this time."

"I'm really not sure what you mean," she told him. "I think -"

Before she could get another word out, she saw the man's face. As he looked at her, she realized that he appeared impossibly pale and gaunt, as if his skin was clinging to his skull with no fat beneath it at all. His eyes, in particular, seemed to be almost bulging from their sockets, glaring with an intensity that she had never before witnessed.

"I think you should leave," she said, although she immediately heard the fear in her own voice. "Do you understand me? If you have business with my father, you can return when -"

"You must not stay in this place," he replied, interrupting her. "She won't like it."

"I've already told you that I don't understand," she stammered. "I'm not comfortable with you being here, so will you please -"

"Have you seen her?" he asked.

She opened her mouth to tell him again that he had to go, but at the last second she held back. She had, in truth, seen a strange woman several times now at the house, although she had no idea how some strange country yokel would know such things.

"You have," he continued. "I see it in your eyes. You know who I'm talking about."

"I'm sure I do not," she said defiantly.

"You know you shouldn't be here," he told her. "She will not tolerate you for much longer. She's used to having this place all to herself, and she will not like intruders."

He looked past her, watching the house with a growing sense of fear.

"I can sense her from here," he added. "She is not a bad woman, at least she was not when she was alive. She made a mistake, but we all make mistakes. Since that night, however, something has changed in her. She is bitter about the way that her life ended."

"You're not making any sense at all," Patience replied. "Sir, please, my father will be back soon and you should be gone by that time. He will not like you loitering on our property."

"I can do no more than warn you," he said, turning to her again, and now there appeared to be small holes around his eyes, as if something had burrowed into what remained of his skin. "If you do not heed that warning, I can no longer help you." He tilted his head slightly, and now his eyes began to blacken. "I believe she learned from poor Catherine," he added, as his voice darkened considerably. "She learned so much, and now she will do whatever it takes to drive you all out. Either that, or she will takes what she wants from you."

"I don't know what -"

"She is at one of the windows now."

Turning, Patience looked at the house. She half expected to spot her mother, but instead she saw only the bare windows of the house reflecting the forest and the sky. At the same time, she somehow felt as if there *should* be someone there, someone who was managing to stay hidden and unseen.

"Don't let her destroy your family," the man said. "She was good once, but now... now she is not."

"I don't know who you're talking about," Patience replied, still watching the house for a moment before turning back to him. "Do you mean the woman I saw at -"

In that instant she realized that the man was gone. She looked all around; there was no way he could possibly have walked away so quickly, especially without making a sound, yet there was no sign of him. A moment later a chill wind blew against her, and Patience told herself that there was really no need to worry *where* the man had gone. All that mattered was that he was no longer around, so after a few more seconds she turned and began to make her way back toward the house.

She couldn't help glancing over her shoulder a couple of times, just to be really sure that the man had disappeared. By the time she reached the pile of wood again, she had just about managed to convince herself that all was right with the world again.

CHAPTER FOURTEEN

"I HOPE FATHER HAS the other chimney fixed soon," Patience said that evening, as she knelt in front of the hearth in the study and warmed her hands against the fire she'd spent some time building. "This house is liable to become very cold at night if he does not."

She turned to her mother, who was sitting on a chair by the desk.

"Half of it, at least," she added with a faint smile, hoping to raise a similar reaction from Rose. "Don't you think so, Mother? We're going to suffer in the winter if the house just has all these holes in it. But Father will have thought of that, won't he?"

Instead of replying, Rose merely stared across the room, watching the far corner just as she had been doing for a while now. Patience followed her gaze and saw only an old chair that – until that moment – she had barely noticed at all. The chair was upholstered in some kind of dark green fabric, and although it stood empty there was nevertheless something about this emptiness that held Patience's attention for longer than she had expected. Indeed, the more she watched this particular chair, the more she felt as if the emptiness was staring back at her.

"Do you see something?" Rose asked.

Patience turned to her.

"In that chair?" Rose continued, still watching the chair with a puzzled expression. "Sometimes I think, just for a moment..."

Her voice trailed off.

"What do you think, Mother?" Patience asked. "What do you see?"

"Do not tell your father when he returns," she replied, "but sometimes, just for a moment, I think there might be somebody there."

"Where?"

Patience turned to look at the chair again.

"In that thing?"

"It's not that I have seen anyone," Rose continued. "Far from it. Yet, I have a growing conviction that I *shall* see someone, or at least... that there is someone I ought to see. That something is wrong with me if I do not see her."

"Her?" Patience replied quickly, picking up on the use of that particular word.

"Again, I do not know why I think such a thing," Rose said, and now she sounded almost as if she was in a trance. "I am not explaining myself well, I know that, but I have been contemplating the empty space in that chair for some hours now, and I am increasingly convinced that it is in some manner not empty at all."

"I think it must be," Patience said, before getting to her feet and walking over to the chair. She took a moment to wave her hand through the empty space, and then she turned to her mother. "See? I do not perceive anybody here."

"You should not stand so close," Rose told her.

"What if I sit in it?" Patience asked, before doing just that. The seat creaked and groaned beneath her weight, as if it was old and barely able to support any weight at all. "How -"

"Get out!" Rose shrieked, suddenly leaping to her feet and rushing across the room. "Do not sit there!"

Startled, Patience watched as her mother reached out with bandaged hands, trying to pull the chair. Resisting at first, Patience quickly saw that her mother's bandages were slipping off, revealing the bloodied, blistered wounds beneath.

"Stop!" Patience gasped, standing up immediately and trying to push her mother away. "Mother, you're going to cause yourself more harm and -"

Before she could finish, Rose grabbed her by the arm and heaved her out of the way, causing her to trip and fall. Stumbling back, Patience tried to stay upright but she quickly fell, landing just a couple of feet from the edge of the roaring fireplace.

"Mother?" she shouted, shocked by Rose's reaction. "Your hands!"

Rose opened her mouth to say something, but instead she merely stood in front of the chair. Her hands, meanwhile, were now torn and bleeding, and the ruptured blisters were leaking some kind of clear liquid that dripped down onto the floorboards. Instead of showing any sign of pain, however, Rose simply stood and stared down at the chair as if she was utterly captivated by the sight of its emptiness.

"Mother?" Patience said cautiously, getting to her feet and stepping closer, while preparing herself to pull back again if necessary. "What is troubling you?"

"Do not sit in that chair," Rose said a little breathlessly, before turning and glaring at her with fearful eyes. "Ever! Do you understand me, my child? You must never even go near that chair ever again!"

***

"She must see a physician," Patience said later, as

she stood with her father in the kitchen. She took a moment to stir the pot of vegetables. "Her hands are -"

"Her hands are healing," Samuel said, interrupting her. He was looking through a tattered book at the table over on the far end of the room. "There is no more to it than that."

"She did more damage to them today," Patience continued. "I replaced the bandages as best I could, but I fear the original wounds are going to become infected. Father, she is not taking good care of her own health and I worry that she will only get worse."

She waited for a reply, but his silence suggested that he had no indication of even considering the matter. In the circumstances, however, she felt that she had no right to keep pushing, since she knew full well that her father's word on all matters was final.

"A man came to the house today," she continued. "A strange fellow he was, too. He had only one arm."

"Is that so? I hope he wasn't looking for work."

"In truth, I know not what he wanted, for he simply spoke for a few minutes about the house itself. You will laugh, Father, but he warned us about some imagined woman he seemed to believe might be living here." She took a moment to stir the vegetables some more; she wanted to know how her father would react to the news about the man, for she couldn't help wondering whether he himself had noticed anything strange in the house. “He was poor, that much I could tell,” she explained, “and he had the most alarming countenance. I would almost go so far as to say that the poor man seemed diseased.”

“Then I hope he did not enter the house,” Samuel said absent-mindedly.

“He did not even approach the door. He was mostly over at the far end of the garden, near the oak tree.”

“Do not worry yourself about any of this,” Samuel told her, still not looking up from the book. “I'm sure he was just some wandering fool who will be long gone by now. I certainly have no intention of giving the matter another thought, not when I have so much other work to do. Mr. Wallace's notes are an awful mess, and I fear it will take me some time to even untangle all the threads of his interests.”

“Can I help in any way?”

“Your mother would usually go over things with me,” he explained, “but she is in no fit state to do so now.”

“Perhaps I might take her place?”

“It would take me as long to teach you, as it would for me to do the work myself. Thank you for offering, however. There will come a time when I shall engage your assistance more fully."

"I am only too glad to help," she told him, although she bristled a little as she realized how meek she sounded. "I fear that Mother will be incapacitated for quite some time."

"You are right," he replied. "The writing *is* terrible."

Puzzled, she turned and saw that he was still looking at the book.

"What did you say?" she asked.

He glanced up at her.

"The writing," he continued matter-of-factly. "You just pointed out that it is an awful scrawl, and you are absolutely correct."

"I said no such thing about -"

Stopping suddenly, she found herself wondering how her father could be so mistaken. Yet again, however, she felt that it was not her place to correct him, and she supposed that perhaps he was simply too engrossed in his work to hear her properly. In that case, she told herself quickly that she should avoid troubling him, and that she should instead focus on preparing a proper hearty meal.

"I'm sorry," she said with a smile, "I should not trouble you with this incessant peppering of questions."

"Quite right," he replied, looking back down at the book. "I'm sorry, Patience, but I'm going to be very busy for the next few days. With your mother unable to work, I'm afraid that much of the burden of keeping the house running will fall onto your young shoulders."

"I shall do my very best to keep you happy," she told him.

"Yes, I think so too," he murmured. "And if it *does* rain, I won't have much choice, I'll just have to get wet."

Patience opened her mouth to ask what he meant, but at the last second she held back. She supposed that she hadn't quite understood his meaning but that she really ought to remain quiet while he worked. And as she continued to stir the soup, she realized that she could hear her mother humming softly in one of the other rooms; this seemed to Patience to be a good thing, almost as if finally Rose was starting to feel a little better.

CHAPTER FIFTEEN

STILL SITTING IN THE study, Rose stared straight ahead and smiled as she heard footsteps heading up the stairs.

"Don't stay up too late, Mother," Patience called down to her. "Father has already retired, and I shall go to my own room now. You should get to bed soon and rest."

Humming gently, Rose failed to even respond. She'd been in her own world for much of the evening, barely even acknowledging anything that was said to her; instead she had been almost exclusively staring at the chair in the corner while humming a variety of tunes that she remembered from her childhood. Although she had managed – just about – to answer direct questions when they had been posed by her husband and daughter, for the most part she had remained lost in her own thoughts.

A moment later she heard Patience's door bump shut upstairs, and a fraction of a second later Rose slowly got to her feet.

"Well, that's quite enough of that, isn't it?" Rose said under her breath, to nobody in particular. She took a moment to fold one of the spare bandages that her daughter had left crumpled on the table. "We can't have this, can we?" she continued. "Everything must be left perfectly tidy, lest more work is made for others."

She glanced briefly at the chair in the corner again, and for a moment a sense of unease crossed her face.

"I wouldn't want that," she added cautiously. "To leave work for others, I mean. One likes to be helpful, does one not? I'm sure anyone with any consideration whatsoever would agree wholeheartedly."

Humming again, she shuffled out into the hallway and made her way toward the kitchen. A faint smile lingered on her face as she headed to the back door. Once she was outside in the cold night air, she ignored her own shivers and shuffled carefully over to a pile of ropes that had been left on the ground. She reached down and began to examine these ropes, assessing them each in turn until finally she picked one up and decided that it was perfectly suitable. At that moment she switched her hum, picking a song that she remembered her own mother singing back in London.

Once she'd separated the rope fully from the others, she made her way back into the kitchen, taking care to shut the back door quietly so as to avoid disturbing anyone. She walked through to the hallway and began to head up the stairs, and now she stopped humming as she realized that she really didn't want either Samuel or Patience to hear that she was up to something. She felt that she had caused them quite enough trouble already, and more than anything she simply wanted now to come up with a nice surprise for the morning.

Stopping at the top of the stairs, she looked around and tried to work out the logistics of her little plan. She wasn't exactly sure how to go about things, but she supposed that she would be able to work something out. Finally, spotting a useful-looking beam high above, she pulled a chair closer from one of the other rooms and climbed up, and then she carefully threaded the rope over the beam and tied it securely in place.

She hesitated, listening to make sure that nobody else in the house was stirring, and then – with a large grin still on her face – she began to tie the rope's other end into the shape of a noose. She had to make several attempts, since she had never done anything like this before, but finally she achieved what she supposed must be the right shape and she promptly set it around her own neck. All the while, she could still hear the pleasant song from her childhood running through her thoughts; in fact, this song was so loud in her head now, it was almost pushing all other considerations away entirely.

Beneath her feet, the chair let out a faint splitting sound, as if it was starting to struggle with her weight.

After adjusting the knot, Rose looked up at the beam again and saw that it was solid. She knew that there was really no need to wait, but the song was continuing in her head and she rather wanted to let it get to its end. She remained tottering on the chair. The song was taking her back to her childhood days, when she used to run around getting under her mother's feet; her mother was long dead, of course, but Rose could still remember her face and her voice, and somehow these memories seemed more alive than ever before. She could almost smell her mother's cooking.

And then the song began to fade, and the smile left Rose's lips as she realized that there was no time for another. She hesitated, wondering whether she might be able to manage one more short song, and then she swallowed hard as she began to understand that the time had come to set up the nice surprise for Samuel and Patience. She imagined how happy they would be in the morning, and deep down she knew that she was doing the best thing for them both. She only wished that she could be around to hear their howls of delight, but she realized that this was impossible.

The time had come.

She hesitated for a few more seconds, and then she stepped off the chair and let herself drop.

As soon as the noose tightened around her neck, she knew that something was wrong. She let out a faint gasp and reached up to touch the rope, and while she'd assumed that death would come instantly, she instead found herself merely struggling for air as she hung high above the stairs. The beam above creaked slightly but show no sign that it might break, yet as Rose tried to pull free from the rope she knew that she was going to have to find some other way to end her own life.

Reaching out, she was about to grab the railing next to the stairs when she suddenly felt hands grabbing her ankles from below.

Startled, she looked down and saw to her horror that a strange woman was standing in the hallway, reaching up and starting to pull on her legs. The woman's face was filled with fury, as if she was horrified by the mere sight of Rose, but after a moment she began to pull harder and harder, cutting off Rose's supply of air completely.

"No!" Rose tried to gasp, suddenly realizing that perhaps her plan had been hasty. Indeed, she was no longer quite sure how she had ended up hanging from the beam at all.

She tried to cry out to Samuel for help, but now she found that she could barely make a sound at all. A moment later she felt something tugging on her feet, and when she looked down she saw that the frightful woman was now pulling repeatedly and hard, as if attempting to hasten her demise.

"Samuel!" she tried to shout, even though she could only manage the faintest whisper. "Help me!"

"Do you think he'll help you?" the woman hissed. "Do you think *anyone* will help you? Even if they heard you, they wouldn't come to help! What use is a woman with no hands?"

As Rose tried again to break free, her bandages began to fall away. Until that moment, the pain had been mostly hidden from her mind, but now it returned as torn flesh and blisters hung from her fingers and knuckles.

"Help me!" she whimpered. "Why are you doing this to me?"

"You can't look after your husband!" the woman sneered, still pulling hard on Rose's feet. "What use could he possibly have for you?"

"You don't know anything!" Rose gasped. "Please, you have to let me go!"

Now the woman below was snarling at her, clearly furious at her refusal to die. Rose tried to twist first one way and then the other, but she could not break free and instead she felt a sharp pain growing in the back of her neck. She looked up at the beam, praying that it might snap, but she quickly saw that it remained as strong as ever. She just had time for one last prayer to the Lord, begging for release, before her body was pulled again and her neck snapped.

Now Rose hung silently and still, dangling from the rope in the darkness of the stairway. Her dead eyes were wide open, staring up toward the beam, and her mouth had been left in a silent scream.

Indeed, the whole of Hadlow House stood in utter silence until, a few minutes later, the chair on the corner of the study was briefly heard creaking – as if someone had just sat down.

CHAPTER SIXTEEN

STUMBLING OUT FROM THE front door, Patience almost tripped on the step as she staggered onto the mud and dropped to her knees. As morning light shone down, she stared straight ahead for a moment and tried to rid her mind of the awful sight.

A few seconds later, her father stepped out behind her.

"Why?" Patience stammered. "Father, why would she..."

After pausing for a moment, she turned to him. Before she could say a word, however, she spotted her mother's body resting in the hallway, covered by the coat that Samuel had just that moment put in place.

"Why would she do something like that?" Patience sobbed. "Why didn't we stop her?"

"There's no sense dwelling on it now," Samuel said calmly, staring off into the distance. "What's done is done."

"Are you sure she's dead?" Patience asked, even as she thought back to the sight of her mother's pale, lifeless face. "Should we check again?"

"She's dead, alright," Samuel replied, "and there's no arguing with that. All that's left is to find a grave for her." He looked around. "I can't afford the cemetery," he added, "but we'll be able to make something nice here."

"But why would she end her life?" Patience whispered, getting to her feet even thought she felt her knees might buckle at any moment. "Father, this makes no sense. Is it possible that I'm dreaming?"

"Your mother was a good woman," Samuel told her, "but she had her weaknesses. She'll have to explain herself to her maker, and those who take their own lives are usually condemned to -"

He stopped himself just in time.

"Well," he continued, "there's no point troubling ourselves about that now. As I said, what's done is done, and all that's left is for her to be laid to rest. I shall see if I can speak to the priest today. Although, now I think about it, that is no great task. Patience, you must go into the village and find Father Ward at St. Leonard's, and ask for his advice. Then you will relay that advice to me. Do you understand?"

"Father," she replied, shaking her head as tears ran down her face, "is this our fault? Is there something else we should have done for her?"

"Go to Cobblefield," he said firmly, "and speak to Father Ward. While you are gone, I shall clean up the mess your mother has left here."

***

"But why would your mother do such a thing?" Daniel asked, as he and Patience sat in the barn in the village. "Did she give you any suggestion that she might be contemplating..."

His voice trailed off, as if he couldn't quite bring himself to finish that sentence.

"None at all," Patience replied, as more tears ran down her face. "Father woke and found her hanging there. I heard a commotion and went out of my room to see what was wrong, and I saw him trying to get her down. That's when I spied her face and..."

She hesitated as she thought back to her mother's horrified final expression. The image was burned into her mind, and she couldn't shake the feeling that she might never be able to forget such a sight ever again. What if, she wondered, she was doomed now to spend the rest of her life reliving that terrible moment over and over again?

Suddenly Daniel leaned close and hugged

her tight.

"I'm so sorry," he told her. "If I could do anything to change this, I would."

"No-one can," she replied, and she had to admit – to herself, at least – that she liked the sensation of his arms wrapped around her. "Whatever demon filled her thoughts at the end, at least she is no longer suffering. I hope not, anyway, but do you think she might have gone to Hell?"

"Don't think about that."

"Yes, but -"

Before she could finish, she saw a young girl – no more than fifteen or sixteen years old – stepping into the large open doorway. In her left hand, the girl was holding what appeared to be a rag-doll.

"Daniel?" the girl said cautiously. "Who is this?"

"Anne," Daniel replied, pulling away from the hug as if he'd been caught doing something wrong, "I didn't hear you coming." He got to his feet and took a step back. "Anne, this is Patience from Hadlow House. Patience, this is my little sister."

"Why are you upset?" Anne asked.

"It's nothing," Patience replied, wiping the tears away as she got to her feet. "I should get going, I have errands to run and Father will want me home soon."

"I'll walk with you," Daniel said.

"You really don't need to."

"No, it's fine," he replied, before reaching out and taking hold of her hand. "I'd like to."

Feeling a little embarrassed, Patience pulled her hand away before looking over at the girl.

"That's a pretty doll," she told her. "Is it yours?"

"Her name's Elizabeth," Anne said cautiously. "Like the old queen who died a long time ago."

"She takes that silly doll with her wherever she goes," Daniel said, rolling his eyes, "even though I frequently tell her that she's far too old for such things. Honestly, sometimes I think she believes it to be a real baby!"

"I do not!" Anne protested angrily. "You don't know what you're talking about, Daniel. Why do you always have to say stupid things all the time?"

With that, she turned and stomped away, taking the doll with her.

"I love my sister," Daniel told Patience, "but I'm not blind to the fact that she can be a little childish for her age. Father dotes on her, most likely because our mother died while she was giving birth to her."

"I'm sorry," Patience told him.

"There's no need," he replied. "If being

sorry could bring her back, then I'd be the sorriest man in all the world, but there's really not much to be gained. I go to my mother's grave every so often and make sure she has some flowers. She loved flowers, so that seems right somehow. It's all I can do for her."

"Do you ever -"

Patience stopped herself just in time.

"Do I ever what?" he asked.

She shook her head.

"Do I ever see her?" he continued. "Is that what you were going to ask? If I ever see her as a ghost?"

"I'm sorry," she replied, "I really meant it when I said that I should go?"

"I've never seen her as a ghost," he explained, "but I believe that to be a good thing. The way I reckon, the souls of those who are content in death go to some other place. It's the ones who are tormented who stay, the ones who have some unfinished business in this world. That's why I think Hadlow House might be haunted, on account of what happened there all those years ago."

"I think I have seen that woman twice now."

"But your parents have never said anything about her?"

She shook her head again.

"There's an atmosphere in that place," he continued, "one that I do not believe to be healthy.

I'm not suggesting that this contributed to what happened to your mother, but I'm not ruling it out either." He hesitated yet again, before reaching out and placing a hand on the side of her arm. "I worry about you being there, Patience," he added. "I worry about what will happen to you, and to your family. You heard that scream the other night, it wasn't natural."

"My parents didn't hear it."

"That only makes things worse," he suggested. "I think you should try to persuade your father to take you away from Hadlow House. What happened to your mother should be a sign to both of you that the place is no good. I know you've seen enough to understand what I mean, Patience. Some presence from the past is still in the house and I think it means you harm."

"Are you sure you're not getting a little ahead of yourself?" she asked awkwardly, and now her voice betrayed the fear she felt in her heart. "Father says that I can be very impressionable, and he might be right. I thought I saw that woman but -"

"Do you doubt your own eyes now?" he replied, cutting her off. "Never do that, Patience. You have to always believe what you see with your own two eyes."

"I should go," she told him, pulling away from his touch, suddenly aware that she was perhaps letting him get too close. "Thank you for your concern, but I can't possibly ask my father to leave that house, not when we've only just arrived. We'll simply have to hope that nothing else happens there."

She turned and hurried away, keen to make sure that he couldn't stop her. Even though she hated the idea of returning to Hadlow House, and despite the fear that was churning in her belly, she knew that she had no choice.

CHAPTER SEVENTEEN

"FATHER?" PATIENCE ASKED A couple of hours later, as she stepped across the garden and saw her mother's body resting on a pile of sticks and twigs, beneath a white sheet. "What are you doing?"

"What I should have done from the start," he replied firmly.

"I couldn't find Father Ward," she replied, as she looked at her mother's bare feet and saw that the ankles were thick with bruises, "but I'm sure -"

Before she could finish, flames consumed the corpse. Shocked, Patience could only stare in horror as her father stepped back and the fire began to grow.

"You said you were going to bury her!" she gasped.

"This is quicker and easier," he replied,

staring at the flames. "I'm sorry, Patience, you might not like this but it's really the best way. Your mother never liked being a burden on anyone, so I'm sure she'd understand."

"But a Christian burial is -"

"Speak no more of it!" he snapped angrily, turning to her with pure rage in his eyes. "Do you understand me? I am the man of this house and my decisions are final, and I will not be second-guessed by a mere girl!"

"Of course," she said, pulling back slightly, shocked by his fury. "I'm sorry, Father, I didn't mean to doubt you. I just didn't understand, that's all."

"You're upset about your mother's death," he replied, "and that is clouding your judgment. I understand, but more than ever now I need you to keep the household running. Hadlow House is a large property for just the two of us, Patience, and you're going to have to take on a great deal of responsibility. I shall endeavor to find a housekeeper, but that will take time and for now I need to know that I can rely on you." He waited for an answer. "*Can* I rely on you?"

"Yes," she stammered, before looking at the bonfire again as the flames flickered and crackled. "I'm sorry."

"I shall deal with this," he indicated, nodding toward the funeral pyre. "You must busy yourself with matters inside the house."

"Yes, Father," she replied, before realizing that he was waiting for her to leave. "I'm sorry, Father," she added. "Of course. I won't let you down."

***

Wiping away more tears, Patience picked up some of her mother's old bandages, which had been left on the table in the study. Sniffing, she saw blood on some of the bandages, and she found herself thinking back to the fact that her mother had been alive just twenty-four hours earlier.

Turning to leave the room, she stopped as she spotted some damage to the window. Taking a closer look, she saw that part of the frame had been gnawed away, as if something with large teeth had bitten furiously at the wood. She took a few seconds to clear away a number of sharp fragments, and then – hearing a floorboard creak loudly in the hallway – she looked over her shoulder.

"Father, I -"

Before she could finish, she saw a woman in a gray dress walk past the bottom of the stairs and disappear quickly toward the kitchen.

"Wait!" Patience called out, hurrying to the door but immediately seeing that the hallway was now empty.

Looking around, she felt absolutely certain that nobody could have simply disappeared so quickly. She waited, trying to work out whether the strange woman might have somehow gone into the dining room, but the house was almost oppressive in its silence and stillness, and after a few seconds Patience took a step forward. As she did so, her left foot pressed against a loose board, immediately causing the exact same creaking sound that had rung out just a few seconds earlier.

"Hello?" Patience said cautiously. "Can you hear me? Is there anybody there?"

As the silence persisted, she already felt certain that she would receive no reply. Nevertheless, after a moment she walked over to the next door and looked into the dining room, and then she walked into the kitchen and stopped again. Looking around, she waited for any hint that the woman in the gray dress might have returned, and then she carefully set the soiled bandages down on a nearby table.

"I've seen you a few times now," she continued, hoping to perhaps spur the figure into making a reappearance. "Just little moments. I don't know your name, but you must be someone who has a strong history with this house. Are you..."

She hesitated, but she quickly reminded herself that she needed to be brave.

"Are you Mrs. Hadlow?" she asked, taking a

step forward.

Silence.

"Are you the former housekeeper?" she continued. "I'm afraid I don't know your name, if that is indeed who you are. My father mentioned that there was a housekeeper here once, which is only proper."

She stepped over to the middle of the room.

"If you're here, what do you want?" she asked. "I can perhaps help you if only you'll tell me, but you really must give me a little assistance."

Slowly turning, she looked toward the kitchen's far end, yet still there was no sign of the woman. She looked the other way again.

"I met a man outside," she continued, "who might be known to you. I didn't get his name either, I'm afraid, but he had only one arm and -"

Suddenly a cup flew across the room, and Patience saw it only just in time. Pulling back, she let out a gasp as the cup hit the wall nearby and dropped to the floor.

"Who are you?" she called out again, and now her heart was racing. "Are you angry? Is that it? Did you mean to hurt me just now?"

She waited, and she was starting to realize that the merest mention of the one-armed man seemed to have conjured great ire in the heart of this ghostly presence.

"He warned me about you," she continued,

hoping to inspire another reaction. “The one-armed man, I mean. I think it was you he talked about, anyway. He told me that Father and I should leave this place, and he spoke about you as if you are some wicked person. At the time I really wasn't sure what to make of him, but now I fear he was trying to help and I should have asked him some more questions. If he -”

Hearing a clinking sound, she turned and looked over at the counter. One of the cups had fallen over, as if nudged by some unseen force, but at least it hadn't been launched across the room. Patience caught herself wondering whether the strange woman was too weak to attack again, or whether instead she had merely come to better control her anger.

“You're not happy, are you?” she asked, stepping back across the room. “I can feel it now. You're here because some kind of anger compels you to remain, but what exactly do you think can satisfy that anger? I am quite sure that anything that happened to you must have occurred long before my family arrived here at Hadlow House, yet my understanding is that the house itself is not that old. Certainly it cannot be more than, say, half a century since the first brick was laid, so what has occurred in that time to cause you so much anguish?”

She watched the cups, hoping that one would move again to prove that she was getting through to the spirit.

"Why did that one-armed man warn me about you?" she continued, returning to the subject that had triggered the first flash of apparent anger. "Now that I think of him some more, I realize that there was real fear in his eyes. And it would seem that he dares not approach the house, which must mean that even in death has is scared of you. Why would one ghost be afraid of another?"

She waited, letting that question linger in the air and hoping that she might draw out a reaction. A moment later, just as she was about to speak again, she flinched as she heard glass breaking and she turned to see that one pane in the window had cracked. And then, hearing a fluttering sound, she stepped over to the window and saw an injured bird on the grass, desperately trying to fly away despite one broken wing.

Suddenly Samuel stepped into view. He glared at Patience for a moment, before reaching down and picking the bird up. He held it in his hands for a moment, and then – with one swift move – he killed it by snapping its neck.

"I'm sorry, Father," Patience said, turning and hurrying across the kitchen, realizing that she needed to get back to work. "I shall try to remember one of Mother's favorite recipes."

CHAPTER EIGHTEEN

ONE WEEK LATER, PATIENCE and Daniel strolled across a small stone bridge that curved up and over the river, about half a mile from the house.

"You have a lot on your mind today," Daniel told her as they reached the top of the bridge and looked down into the water flowing below. "I can tell."

"Mother's death is still fresh in my mind," she replied uneasily, trying to force a smile. "Father has not been his usual self since she died. I can understand that, of course. I myself have been troubled by many thoughts on the matter, but Father's condition seems different somehow. It's as if he has changed deep down, and I do not know how long it will take him to change back."

"People don't," Daniel said. "Not always."

She turned to him.

"After my mother died," he continued, "everything changed. The whole world, it seemed to me, was different. I was only young, six years old, and I remember waiting for things to go back to normal. For my father to go back to being the man he'd been before. But the truth is, death changes the living, and I do not believe that they often change back. The difference is permanent."

"I hope you're wrong," she told him, "for Father seems to have lost much of his joy in life. He barely smiles, and he never laughs."

"And you?"

"What about me?"

"Do you smile? Do you laugh?"

"I am too busy to do either," she replied. "I know nothing about running a house, other than my memories of seeing my mother hard at work, and I know I am disappointing my father daily. My cooking, for one thing, is rather terrible, no matter how hard I try."

"I'm sure you'll get better," he told her. "After all, it's clear to me that you're exceedingly clever."

"I am no such thing."

"You have something on your nose," he added.

"I do?"

Trying to see what was wrong, she almost

went cross-eyed for a few seconds until Daniel reached up and wiped a muddy finger across her nose's tip.

"Now you do, at least," he told her.

"Hey!"

Stepping back, she laughed as she wiped the mud away, and then – as if she felt that laughing was not appropriate – she forced herself to be more serious.

"You're beautiful when you do that, you know," Daniel continued. "Well, not only when you do that. You're beautiful all the time. Even when you look sad."

"Well, now I know for certain that you are quite demented," she replied, before pausing for a moment. "Father still does not want me to spend time with you," she added cautiously, "but I confess that I would like to come for another walk again soon. Even if it is only brief, since I cannot be away from the house for long, I should very much like to have something to look forward to."

"How about tomorrow?" he asked. "I can meet you at the same place, at the same time."

"I don't know that I shall be able to get away."

"Then we shall say it in this manner," he replied. "Every day I shall wait on this bridge, at this time. If you are able to come, then come. If you are not able, I shall understand, but I shall be here every day regardless. How does that sound?"

"It sounds too much for me to ask of you," she said, smiling even as she felt tears welling in her eyes. "But I am too grateful to turn down your kind offer, so I must accept."

***

"Hadlow House does not look so bad in the daytime," Daniel pointed out a short while later, as he and Patience stopped at the side of the dirt track that led to the front gate. "I'd even go so far as to say that it looks rather... nice."

"We should go no further right now, she told him, "in case my father sees us together."

"Am I that much of a bad influence on you?"

"Apparently so," she said with a smile, before pausing for a moment. "Daniel, if I tell you something, do you promise that you won't think that I'm terribly foolish."

"I could not think such a thing ever."

"I have tried several times over the past week to... anger whatever ghost lives in the house."

"What do you mean?"

"I have done small things that I hoped would draw it out," she explained. "There is a spirit in there, it is a woman and she wears a gray dress. There are certain things I say that I believe make her angry, but apart from one brief burst of rage I have been rather unsuccessful in my endeavors."

"Why would you do such a thing?" he asked.

"To see her. To talk to her. To find out what keeps her here."

"You should not meddle with things you don't understand," he pointed out. "Have you not considered the possibility that by acting as you do, you inadvertently contribute to the anger that makes her stay?"

"I have thought of that," she told him, "but she was here already, so I do not believe I have such power. I merely wish to commune with her so that I can perhaps help to set her free. And since anger appears to be her primary emotion, I thought -"

"Don't do this, Patience," he said firmly.

"You haven't heard the entirety of my plan yet."

"I don't need to," he replied. "If there's a ghost at Hadlow House – and I'm fairly sure we both know that *something's* not right in there – you mustn't meddle. We don't have a clue what you might be facing, so the only option is to let it be. Do you understand me? Let this thing rest and don't provoke it."

"I only -"

"No excuses," he continued, placing his hands on the sides of her arms. "This is important,

Patience. You might think that you can involve yourself with such matters, but you risk bringing a terrible calamity upon yourself. Only thirty or so years have passed since a man committed multiple murders at this house."

"If you're talking about Mr. Hadlow," she replied, "then we really don't know exactly what happened. He might not have killed anyone at all."

"I'm not taking any chances," he told her. "Patience, if something's rotten in this house, then you must let it be. Try to ignore it, and hope that it in turn ignores you too. That's the only way to deal with such things. With any luck, after a while this spirit will fade to nothing." He paused, looking deep into her eyes as he tried to determine whether or not she was taking his advice seriously. "I can't stand the thought that you might be in danger," he added, "and that something might happen to you. Patience, please, be sensible and leave this thing alone. Do you promise me?"

She opened her mouth to argue with him, but at the last moment she realized that there was no point.

"This spirit could do you harm," he reminded her.

"I shall mind your words," she replied, "and act accordingly. You need not worry. But don't you think that it's men, not spirits, that cause the most harm?"

"I would not like to tempt either," he said with a heavy sigh. "Are we agreed? Do you promise that you will no longer make any attempt to draw this thing out?"

"I promise," she muttered, although she was unable to hide a sense of irritation. "Are you happy now? I promise to be a good little girl and do as I'm told. Indeed, I would never dream of causing trouble, and I hope that you are satisfied now." She glanced over her shoulder. "My father will be home soon," she added, "and as I have mentioned already, it would be wise if you are not here."

"Of course," he said, letting go and taking a step back. "Remember my promise about the bridge, Patience. I shall wait for you there every day, and I hope to see you very soon."

"You will, I am sure," she replied with a smile and perhaps even the first hint of a blush. "I shall try tomorrow, and if I fail in that, I shall try the next day and the next. Truly, Daniel, the thought of seeing you again might be the only thing that gets me through these days of drudgery. I know I must help my father, and I do so willingly, but just a few minutes of escape would mean the world to me."

"I shall be there," he said, turning and walking away. "But mind what I told you just now," he called back to her. "Promise me you will not make any more attempts to contact the ghost in that house!"

"I promise!" she replied with a smile. "You have my word on that, Daniel!"

As those words left her lips, she had one hand behind her back; and on this hand, she had her index and middle fingers firmly crossed.

CHAPTER NINETEEN

"THE WEATHER SEEMS TO be taking a turn for the worse," Patience observed as she made her way around the dining room table and picked up the dirty plates. "I fear that tonight there will be rain and high wind."

Her father managed only a faint grunt in response. As she walked toward the door, Patience caught sight of him reflected in one of the windows and she couldn't help but notice – not for the first time that night – that he seemed lost entirely in a world of his own. As she stepped out into the hallway, she told herself that it was not her place to bother him, but she couldn't stop turning to look once more.

"You know you can talk to me, Father," she said after a moment's hesitation. "If there's anything on your mind, I am -"

"Don't you have dishes to clean?" he asked gruffly, still simply staring straight ahead.

"I do," she replied. "I'm sorry. I shall get to work at once."

Still she hesitated, however, and one matter was at that moment weighing heavily upon her conscience.

"I wanted to ask you about Mother," she continued, "and -"

"Your mother's body has been laid to rest."

"It has?"

"It has."

"Might I ask where?"

"That is of no importance."

"Did you bury her here? Is she in the garden?"

"Patience, you do not understand such things," he told her. "I saw no need to involve you, for there was a risk that you would only cause trouble. The fact of the matter, which you must accept, is that I have disposed of your mother's earthly remains in a dignified and respectful manner. She is with the Lord now."

"Might I visit her grave?"

"You might not," he said firmly. "You would only get upset."

"But -"

"And I will not have that," he added,

interrupting her. “Patience, do not trouble me further with such concerns. Trust me when I tell you that your mother rests peacefully with the Lord. When you are a little older and a little less emotional, I shall take you to the spot and you shall see that it is quite beautiful.”

“Yes, Father,” she replied, even though she was still rather unhappy about the arrangement. Then again, she knew that he was right and that she could sometimes let her emotions take charge. “I'm sorry for questioning your judgment, Father. I shall not do it again.”

As she made her way through to the kitchen, she felt as if her attempt to elicit any kind of conversation were doomed to failure. Wind rattled the panes of the windows as she set the plates down, and then she paused as she saw the flame of a nearby candle flickering. The bad weather outside, she reasoned, was very much conducive to a sense of eerie isolation within the house itself, and she couldn't help but wonder whether a troubled and restless night might encourage any ghostly spirits to show themselves. In fact, as she turned and looked back across the kitchen, she heard wind whistling through the top of the house and she half expected to once again spot the lady in the gray dress.

A moment later, hearing footsteps, she realized that her father was making his way through to the study. Sure enough, she heard the by-now familiar sound of that creaking loose floorboard just outside the study door, but something about this particular noise was now rather comforting. She heard her father sitting down, and she was relieved by the sense of his calm, strong presence. Had she been alone in the house at that moment, she would most certainly have felt very nervous about possibly seeing the ghostly woman, but with her father around she felt no fear at all. She told herself that no matter what happened, her father would always keep her safe.

Always.

"Are you here now?" she whispered, even though she knew that Daniel would be furious if he found out that she was trying again to contact the spirit. "It's okay if you are. I just want to know."

The back door rattled now, buffeted by the wind, but this only served to accentuate the calm silence of the house. A moment later, just as she was about to try talking to the ghost again, Patience realized that she could hear the faintest of murmurings coming from one of the other rooms. She made her way to the door and looked past the side of the staircase, and in that moment she was just about able to make out her father's voice.

"I know," he was saying. "You're right. She's just a young girl, really, and she's having to grow up so fast."

Taking a deep breath, Patience felt tears in

her eyes. She'd always known her father as a strong, stoic type of man, but now evidently he was having his own whispered conversation with his dead wife. Patience's first thought was that she should go to him and offer some words of comfort, but instead she held back as she realized that she really didn't want to interrupt what seemed to be a moment of genuine happiness.

"Yes," he continued, "you're right. She has a lot to learn, but so far she has surprised me greatly. Even her cooking has improved, which is surely a miracle."

Patience smiled as a solitary tear ran down her left cheek.

"Is that so?" her father added. "I'm really not sure that I see it that way. She works hard as it is, I do not believe that I need to discipline her any further."

Surprised by the turn the conversation was taking, Patience swallowed hard.

"Perhaps you are right," Samuel continued. "Sometimes I worry that she is becoming too wild. But do you really think the way she talks to me is so bad?"

Patience waited for his next works.

"Very well," he murmured. "I shall do so. I'm sure that, as ever, you are absolutely correct."

After a few seconds of silence, Patience took a step back. She was shocked by her father's words, and by the thought that he would imagine such a conversation with her mother, but she quickly told herself that she merely needed to stick to her work and wait for the next time she might be able to meet Daniel. Even the thought of him waiting on the little stone bridge filled her heart with joy, and as she made her way back to the counter and began to once again deal with the various dishes, she tried to work out whether she might be able to get to the bridge on the following day.

***

Outside, a few hundred meters from the house, two men trudged through the undergrowth. Their feet pressed against the dead leaves on the ground, but they made no effort to stay quiet and after a moment their dog raced past and hurried breathlessly past the edge of the clearing. The evening light was low, casting the men as little more than dark silhouettes as the wind picked up and a few spots of rain began to fall.

"You don't think the new people at Hadlow House'll mind us being out here, do you?" James asked. "The place has been empty for so long, but technically this *is* their land."

"I don't see any reason how they'll ever know," his fellow poacher John replied. "They certainly won't be missing a few rabbits here and there, that's for sure. Besides, I heard that this Butler fellow's not exactly the most observant of men, so we should be alright."

Hearing the dog bark up ahead, he stopped for a moment to get his bearings before setting off again, picking a slightly different direction this time.

"Sounds like the hound's already onto something," he continued. "We might be home before the truly bad weather sets in after all."

"That'd be a blessing," James muttered, pulling his coat a little closer as he followed. "If you ask me, it's a crime that all this land is sitting unused, just because whoever's in Hadlow House hasn't got the time to use it. How would they feel if it was left to go wild? I'm sure they'd soon be complaining about it all being grown over."

"You're not wrong there," John said as the dog barked again. "What's up with that animal, anyway? He likes his rabbits, that's for sure, but he's not usually *this* excited."

They walked along in silence for a few more minutes, picking their way through increasingly thick and knotty undergrowth as they approached the eastern edge of Hadlow House's grounds. This was a particularly untouched past of the estate, where even the poachers rarely ventured, but times were hard and James and John were sturdy fellows who didn't much mind a challenge. They could hear the dog up ahead now, frantically pawing at something, and James had already reached for his bag in anticipation of one or two of the traps being filled with rabbits. And then, as he emerged from behind another bush, James stopped and saw that the dog was sniffing at an object that was most certainly larger than a rabbit.

"What's that, then?" John asked, having stopped just behind him.

"I'm not sure that I know," James replied, tilting his head slightly. "Damn this light, it's almost impossible to make anything out at all."

"What have you got there?" John called out to the dog, as he made his way over. "Come on, get out of the way and let me see."

The dog ignored him, preferring instead to paw with increasing agitation at the large shape on the ground. After a moment, John reached down and grabbed the animal's back legs, hauling him out of the way with such force that a brief yelp rang out. Still, the dog – which had never been troubled by a name, or by any real show of affection – knew better than to argue with the master who occasionally fed him scraps, and he slunk away before turning to watch proceedings.

"What is it?" James asked, stepping closer.

"I think..."

As his eyes adjusted a little better to the

darkness, John was finally able to make out the shape, and after a moment he took a step back. Before him, dumped on the forest floor, was the naked and bloodied corpse of a dead woman; her glassy eyes were wide open, as was her mouth, and thick bruises marked a ring around her neck. She had been tossed aside into the dirt with such lack of care that her legs had been left wide apart, exposing her full nakedness, and beetles had begun to crawl across her scratched rump.

CHAPTER TWENTY

THE FOLLOWING MORNING, STOPPING in the doorway, Patience realized that her father was once again communing with the spirit of her dead mother.

"Do you think so?" he murmured. "I had hoped that she might have learned her lesson."

Taking a step forward, Patience looked into the study and saw that her father was on his knees. This unusual position for a man of his stature was compounded by the way he stared up at the empty chair in the corner, as if he truly believed that Rose was sitting in that spot. Patience opened her mouth to ask whether he was hungry, but at the last second she held back. Evidently Samuel had not noticed her approach, and when she saw the side of his face she marked that he seemed almost lost in a spell.

"She has always had a spirited streak," Samuel continued. "I have known that since she was first able to walk and talk."

Patience allowed herself a faint smile.

"If you say so," Samuel added, and now he sounded a little troubled. "You are probably right. You usually are and -"

Suddenly the chair creaked loudly.

"She is?" Samuel said, before turning to look at the doorway. As soon as he spotted Patience, he got to his feet. "You are right. She is."

"Father," Patience replied, trying to force a smile even though she now felt a little unnerved by the sight of the empty hair. Did her father truly see her mother sitting there? "I was wondering if you require anything more to eat before you go out to work."

"I am fine," he said, although he sounded a little uncertain, as if he was unhappy at having been caught in his conversation.

Patience looked at the chair again, and she noticed that this part of the study seemed somehow darker than the rest of the room. She told herself that she was simply imagining things, yet the sense persisted and – if anything – began to become a little stronger, as if the light around the chair was somehow being forced away.

"You are not to come in here while I am out," Samuel said, stepping toward her and forcing her out of the room, then pulling the door shut. "Is that understood? I'm serious, Patience. From now on, indeed, you are never to enter that room at all. Not unless I tell you to."

"Absolutely," she replied, although she couldn't help but furrow her brow. "But, Father, might I ask why?"

Samuel turned and looked at the closed door for a moment, almost as if he heard some noise coming from the other side.

"Follow my rules," he added finally. "All of them, and this one most especially. If I find any proof that you have done otherwise, Patience, I shall punish you. I shall perhaps even use a birch cane."

"Of course," she said, shocked by the threat of physical punishment. "I would never disobey you, Father. I strive only to make you happy."

***

A few hours later, with her father having long since departed for a day of touring the local area, Patience stood at the back door and looked at the fruits of her labors so far.

Several of her father's shirts hung from a line in the garden, fluttering gently in the breeze. So far she had managed to wash them and remove all the stains, and she felt rather proud of herself. And then, as she watched, the fluttering stopped as if the breeze had suddenly faded to nothing, and the shirts hang limply.

Still, she supposed that they would dry perfectly well, even without any assistance.

Suddenly a bump rang out, coming from elsewhere in the house. Patience turned and looked over her shoulder, and she realized that her gaze had instantly fallen upon the door to the study, at the far end of the hallway. She hesitated, telling herself that the bump really could have come from anywhere else in the house, yet somehow deep down she knew that the study must surely have been the culprit. Her first thought was to go and check, to make sure that nothing had fallen down, yet her father's words immediately returned to the back of her mind.

"Follow my rules," she heard his voice saying. "All of them, and this one most especially. If I find any proof that you have done otherwise, Patience, I shall punish you. I shall perhaps even use a birch cane."

She was not to go into the study, that much had been made clear, and she had no desire whatsoever to contradict her father's orders. She had no idea *why* he had been so insistent on this point, but she reminded herself that it was not her place to question her father's rules, even if in this case she could think of no good reason why any room in the house should be off-limits.

Turning to make her way back over to the pile of dirty clothes, she stopped after a few paces as she realized that she could hear another noise.

She looked out into the hallway again, and this time she listened to a faint but persistent scratching sound, as if something – an animal, perhaps – had begun to claw frantically at wood. She told herself that she must be mistaken, but after a few more seconds she made her way to the door and looked through once again at the study. That door remained shut, of course, yet now Patience was more sure than ever that there was something on the other side, and that this particular something seemed to be scratching with increasing fury, almost as if...

Almost as if it was trying to attract her attention. As if it was trying to get her to open the door.

Confused, Patience hesitated, not knowing what she should do next. In ordinary circumstances she would of course have gone to the door and pushed it open and investigated the source of the noise, yet her father's words rang clearer than ever in her thoughts.

"I'm serious, Patience," she heard him saying. "From now on, indeed, you are never to enter that room at all. Not unless I tell you to."

After a moment, looking down, she realized that her right hand had inadvertently already reached for the door's handle. She hesitated, wondering whether she might take a quick look just to make absolutely sure that nothing was wrong on the door's other side, and she supposed that her father would never even have to know. At the same time, she had been trying to temper her rebellious side, and to simply obey all his orders and instructions without question. For a moment she felt two sides of her personality pulling against one another, unable to reconcile, but finally – and not without some effort – she pulled her hand back as she realized that she had to be good.

Suddenly the scratching sound stopped.

Patience tilted her head, staring at the door, and she began to wonder whether she could now hear another sound coming from the other side. Was there not, she wondered, the faintest hint of somebody breathing heavily? She leaned a little closer, holding her breath, and the sound continued as if somebody was standing just out of sight on the other side of the door. Although she knew that this was impossible, and that there could be nobody in the room, Patience found herself thinking back to the strange woman in the gray dress. Was it possible that she was waiting in the study?

"Hello?" Patience whispered, although she still did not dare to open the door. "Can... can you hear me?"

She waited, but now the breathing sound

had stopped. A moment later, she heard the telltale sound of the chair in the corner creaking slightly as if under the weight of someone who had just sat down.

"Mother, is that you?" she asked.

No matter how much she wanted to open the door, she knew that she must not. She felt the temptation burning in her chest, and finally she forced herself to step back. Despite the curiosity burning in her chest, she knew that she would feel greater pride by displaying a hitherto hidden degree of obedience. The sound in the room was most likely nothing out of the ordinary, and her father was sure to make everything alright just as soon as he returned home. With that newfound sense of confidence in her heart, Patience turned to go back to the kitchen.

Stopping in her tracks, she saw two bare feet hanging in the air directly in front of her face. Looking up, she saw that her mother's body was hanging once again from the beam, staring down at her with bloodied, bulging eyes. In that moment, all Patience could do was scream.

CHAPTER TWENTY-ONE

"ARE YOU ALRIGHT?"

Standing on the little stone bridge a few hours later, Patience stared down into the water. Several hours had elapsed since she'd dropped sobbing and trembling to the floor at Hadlow House, staring up in horror at the apparition of her mother's corpse hanging above; the figure had appeared for only a few seconds before blinking away, and Patience had just about managed to convince herself that she must have imagined the whole thing, yet somehow that awful sight kept returning unbidden to her thoughts.

"Patience?"

As soon as she felt his touch on her arm, she let out a shocked gasp and pulled away.

"I think that answers my question," Daniel

continued. “You're not yourself today. You know you can talk to me about absolutely anything, don't you?”

“I'm fine,” she lied, and she was immediately conscious that she sounded terribly unconvincing. “What I mean is, I just need a few minutes away from the house to...”

Her voice trailed off, and in truth she was starting to regret showing up at the bridge at all. She'd hoped to take her mind off the strange events in the house, yet instead somehow those awful moments were amplified now that she was alone with Daniel. She looked down at the river again, hoping against hope that the beauty of the water might set her mind at ease, yet now she found herself thinking about the scratching sound on the door. Had some hidden force drawn her into the hallway, with the express intention of making her see her mother's ghost?

She thought, again, of the woman in the gray dress.

“I'm not sure that you should be at that house,” Daniel said after a moment.

She turned to him.

“What do you mean?” she asked.

“I mean that you become a little more fearful every time I see you,” he continued. “Patience, it's evident to me that all isn't well in that place.” He paused. “You spoke before of a spirit.

Have you seen it again?"

"No!" she blurted out, before hesitating. "Yes. No. I don't know."

"And your father -"

"My father communes with my mother," she added, before he could finish. "He is content. She has returned to speak to him, to comfort him from the other side." She swallowed hard. "She does not appear to me, and I can only suppose that is because she thinks I do not need her counsel."

"And what of the other spirit?"

"I don't know!" she snapped, unable to help herself. "Daniel, I feel a headache coming on. You're asking me far too many questions and I simply don't know how to answer."

"Answer with the truth."

"I have done so, to the best of my ability."

"I should like to come to the house with you this morning," he told her. "Your father is out, is he not? Let me come and see what's going on."

She shook her head.

"Why not?" he asked.

"Because it would be wrong," she told him. "I can't invite young gentlemen to the house when I am alone, don't you see how that would look if someone were to find out?"

"My intentions are pure and proper."

"I came out here to spend time with you," she replied, trying to change the subject, "and to get a break from my work at the house. Can't you distract me, Daniel, with talk of something – anything – else? Please, that's all I ask of you today. If you merely remind me of the house, over and over again, then I might as well have just stayed there all along."

He opened his mouth to reply, but at the last second he seemed to understand that there was no point peppering her with yet more questions.

"There was a commotion in the village this morning," he told her finally. "Two poachers found something in the forest, although I don't know what. For once, people are not gossiping. Instead, there are just hushed whispers."

"I'm sure it was nothing," Patience told him, relieved to be talking about a fresh topic. She even managed a faint smile. "Why, I imagine that in a place like Cobblefield, any event is bound to cause great excitement. Please don't take offense, Daniel, but I doubt that many exciting things happen around these parts."

"You're right about that," he replied, and they both turned and looked along the river, and they saw patches of sunlight breaking through the trees. "That's the way I like it, though. I don't think I could cope with a greater pace in life."

***

"She is..."

Father Ward's voice trailed off for a moment as he continued to stare at the awful sight on the table in the back of the public house. Although a cloth sack covered much of the figure's nakedness, the dead woman's face could still be seen, her features frozen in a silent, dead scream.

"Are you saying that you found her like this?" Father Ward continued cautiously, turning to the other men. "Are you saying that she was merely dumped out there in the forest like... waste?"

"That she was," James said, nodding darkly as he too stared at the corpse. "No effort had been made to arrange her in a dignified manner. As you can see, part of her body is very badly burned, and part is not. I have never seen such a terrible thing in all my life."

"And what were you fellows doing out there?" Father Ward asked.

"Walking the dog," John interjected, before James could say another word. "I know there are poachers out on that land sometimes, but we're certainly not up to anything like that."

"Sir, we are not," James said firmly.

"I see," Father Ward murmured, before stepping around the table and looking down at what remained of the woman's face. "It is difficult to make out her features very well, but I take it that she has not yet been recognized."

"She has not," James told him.

"I have not heard of anyone missing from the village," the priest continued. "Word of something like that would soon carry." He paused for a moment, lost in thought. "The body of a loved one would be treated with dignity and care. Conversely, a simple murder victim would be properly hidden. This woman, on the other hand, seems to have been simply thrown away by someone who thought very little on the matter. That's the part that confounds me, really. Was someone trying to hide her corpse or not?"

"We found her near Digger's Dell," James added.

"And what is the significance of that?" Father Ward asked.

"Well, none, not really," James continued. He glanced briefly at John, and then at the priest again. "Well, except for one matter. I'm not sure you're aware of the boundaries, Father Ward, but Digger's Dell happens to be at the very edge of the land occupied by Hadlow House."

"I see. So this woman was placed as far away from that house as possible, while still remaining on the land. As if she might be connected to the place in some manner?"

"It was my first thought, Sir," James said, "although I confess that I am no wise man. That's why we brought her here and had you sent for."

“You were wise to do so,” Father Ward replied, and now he was once again clearly lost in thought. “I've met Mr. Butler from the house, and I happen to know that he has both a wife and a daughter. He is patently a good, honest man, and I cannot imagine that he would ever allow his wife's earthly remains to be left in this manner. Nevertheless, I should perhaps venture out there and pay him a visit, just to ascertain that nothing is the matter.” He thought for a moment longer. “I met his predecessor once, Mr. Hadlow, and I thought that he too was a good man. How wrong I turned out to be on that occasion.”

“Would you like us to come with you?” James asked.

“Hmm?” Father Ward turned to him, as if the idea was utterly absurd. “Oh, no, not at all. Why, I shall merely be paying a visit to one of the more esteemed gentlemen in the vicinity. I am sure that nothing is wrong, I am really only planning to pay him a courtesy visit.” He managed a smile, despite the grotesque figure still resting nearby on the table. “I am sure that this poor dead woman is nothing to do with him. Let me visit the house first, and in the meantime you two can arrange for the body to be prepared for a proper burial.”

CHAPTER TWENTY-TWO

"I'M SO PLEASED TO hear that your work is going well, Father," Patience said as she set a plate of food down in front of him that evening. "From what you've told me, it would seem that you have quite a lot to get done. I had no idea that Mr. Wallace's interests in these parts were so extensive."

"All will be good," Samuel muttered, immediately taking his fork and starting to eat.

"There is no -"

Hearing a bumping sound, Patience let out a shocked gasp and turned to look across the dining room. At the same time she dropped the other plate, letting its contents spill across the floor.

"What is wrong with you?" Samuel asked angrily. "Ever since I returned this evening, you have been so plainly out of sorts."

"I'm sorry," she stammered, as she told herself that the supposed bumping sound must have been something very mundane and normal. Still, from where she was standing, she could just about see past the bottom of the staircase, to the spot where the study's door remained shut. "I suppose I'm just being a little jumpy."

"Your mother knew how to control her emotions," he replied. "You should try to do the same, Patience. Your mother might not be around to teach you, but that does not mean you cannot learn. I do not want to hear too many excuses coming from your lips."

"Of course not," she told him, "and -"

Suddenly she heard a loud knocking sound on the door. Turning, she looked once more out into the hallway, but she knew that this sound was different; to her surprise, she realized that somebody must be at the front door.

"Who would call at such a time?" her father muttered, before watching her for a moment. "Well?" he added, with even more anger than before. "Why are you just standing there. See who has come to visit, and unless it's someone important, have them come back another time. And if you *must* let them inside, then take them to the reception room opposite the study and tell them to wait for me."

She turned to him again.

"Well?" he said again. "Patience, what is wrong with you this evening? Move!"

***

"Hadlow House truly is a wonderful home," Father Ward said as he sat in the front room, looking around at the rather bare furnishings. "I always hoped to come and see the place for myself, but I never managed to do so previously, on account of the..."

His voice trailed off as he turned to look at Samuel, who was sitting on a chair over by the fireplace.

"Well," Father Ward added, "Hadlow House was not occupied for long before it was abandoned for quite some time. Mr. Hadlow -"

"I have heard of this Hadlow gentleman," Samuel said firmly, cutting him off. "He seems to have been quite out of his mind. I do not believe that there is any further benefit to discussion of the man. Tell me, is that why you came out here this evening, or is there some other matter on your mind?"

"There is another matter," the priest said, glancing briefly and somewhat nervously toward Patience before turning to Samuel again. "Your daughter, however, might be too sensitive to hear about such things."

"Patience is no delicate flower," Samuel told him. "She can hear whatever you have to say."

"It's about something that was recently discovered on the edge of your property," Father Ward explained. "Two gentlemen... well, two men who were out there... I'm not sure exactly what they were doing, although they've both assured me that they are not poachers, and as a man of the church I suppose I am inclined to give them the benefit of the doubt, although I have heard many times that -"

"Can we get to the point?" Samuel asked firmly. "If you don't mind?"

"These two men found something rather unfortunate. They chanced upon a body -"

"Patience, you will leave the room!" Samuel said, turning to his daughter. "Now!"

She immediately got to her feet.

"Father, I -"

"Now, Patience!" he boomed. "I have changed my mind. This is not a fit subject for a girl to hear about, so you must busy yourself in the kitchen or better yet you must go upstairs. Do not force me to tell you twice."

"Of course, Father," she replied, looking briefly at Father Ward before hurrying out of the room.

"Shut the door once you are gone!" Samuel boomed.

"Yes, Father."

Once the door was shut, Samuel turned to Father Ward. A moment later they both heard footsteps hurrying up the stairs, indicating that Patience had followed her father's instructions. Samuel hesitated until he heard the door to one of the rooms bumping shut, and then he took a deep breath as he returned his gaze to the priest in the opposite chair.

"You were saying?" Samuel asked cautiously.

"I'm afraid to say that the body of a woman was discovered out there," Father Ward explained, "and -"

"Nobody has any right to be on my land," Samuel told him, interrupting him yet again. "You say that these men are not poachers, yet I fail to see how they can be anything else. I would have their names from you, so that I might set about dealing with this matter."

"Right, well, you see it's not the poaching that -"

"I am responsible for Mr. Wallace's property," Samuel continued, leaning forward in his chair and – in the process – causing it to creak and groan a little beneath his weight, "and I must deal with poaching as and when it arises. You must understand that."

"I do," Father Ward replied, "and I shall give you the names of these men, but I fear you misunderstand the point of my visit this evening. It is not the poaching, exactly, that concerns me, but rather the discovery that these men made out there in the forest. You see, they found the body of a woman, and it seems that she had been left in the most dreadful state. I myself have seen the corpse, and it is quite the most awful thing."

"I fail to see," Samuel said calmly, "how this is any of my concern."

"The woman... *was* found on your property," Father Ward told him. "Technically. I believe so, anyway. It was so close to the boundary, I'm not even sure that the men themselves can be sure, but there is therefore the matter of this life that has been lost."

He paused, waiting for Samuel to reply. A moment later he heard a faint bumping sound coming from out in the hallway, but he kept his gaze fixed firmly on Samuel's face, and now he was starting to realize that the other man's reaction seemed strangely calm and collected.

"Your daughter seems like a good, strong girl," he continued cautiously. "I was wondering, though, about your wife. I heard that you have one, and I just wondered... is she here tonight?"

Again he waited, but he was starting to feel distinctly uneasy and he was having to fight the urge to simply get up and excuse himself from the house altogether.

"Not that I am accusing anyone of untoward actions," he added, forcing a smile. "Mr. Butler, I am quite sure that you are a good man who would never dream of having anything untoward take place on your land or in your family, but I hope you understand that I need to at least ascertain the circumstances behind this..."

His voice trailed off, and now something about Samuel's glare made him feel more troubled than ever.

"But if this is not a good time," he continued, "then I can certainly come back tomorrow. Or the day after. Or I do not even have to come back at all, since I am quite sure that this matter has nothing to do with you!"

Before he could stop himself, Father Ward got to his feet, and now his heart was racing. He desperately wanted to excuse himself from a situation that he could feel getting stranger and stranger with each passing second, yet at the same time he had no desire to offend his host. He waited a moment longer, convinced that Samuel would have to say something eventually, and finally he told himself that he simply needed to leave.

"Well," he said, with the biggest smile he could manage, "perhaps this is a discussion for another day. Do you not think so? It's getting late, and I do not mean to disturb you and your daughter." He paused. "Or your wife."

Still receiving no reply, he hesitated for a few more seconds. And then, as he was about to bid farewell, he heard a clicking sound and he turned just in time to see the door clicking open, revealing not only the hallway but also the door to the room opposite. This door, which led to the study, had been closed when Father Ward had arrived, but now it was wide open and something about the room beyond made the priest feel distinctly uncomfortable. Indeed, after a few seconds he felt a cold shiver run through his bones, and this sensation only made him feel more certain than ever that the time to depart had arrived.

"Well," he continued, turning to Samuel again, "I can only -"

Before he could finish, he felt something cold on his shoulder. He turned to his left and saw to his shock that a pale hand was resting at the top of his arm, and in that moment he realized that somehow there was now a woman standing right behind him, even though he had seen no woman enter the room. He opened his mouth to ask Samuel whether everything was quite alright, but seconds later he felt the woman lean close to his ear from behind, and he heard a slow, cold death rattle emerging from her throat.

CHAPTER TWENTY-THREE

AS SOON AS SHE heard the cracking sound, Patience pulled back from the hole in the fireplace. Since making her way upstairs, she had been kneeling on the floor in the house's master bedroom; the hole in the fireplace, which her father still had not fixed, meant that she had just about been able to make out most of what had been said downstairs, but now the front room seemed to have fallen entirely silent.

She waited, before leaning toward the hole again in an attempt to hear more.

A moment later her father's voice murmured, although she was unable to make out his exact words. She wondered what he might be telling Father Ward; indeed, she still couldn't help but wonder why she had been expelled from the room at all, since there seemed to be no obvious reason why she should be excluded from such a conversation, Then again, she reminded herself that her father was far wiser when it came to these matters, and she reminded herself that she really shouldn't question his decisions. Nevertheless, as the silence stretched out now, she began to wonder when Father Ward was going to respond to whatever her father had just said.

All she heard, a few seconds later, was a faint whispering voice. And this time, the voice most certainly did not belong to her father.

She leaned even closer to the hole, until she was as close as possible, but still she could not make out much detail from this other voice. A woman was speaking, she was fairly sure of that, and after a moment a shudder ran through her chest as she realized that she might be hearing the whispered voice of her own dead mother. Deep down, however, she somehow knew that this was not the case, that the present voice was harsher and more clipped than her mother had ever sounded. She was sure that Father Ward had arrived at the house alone, however, and her thoughts raced for a few seconds before she realized that there was one other possibility.

Pulling back from the hole, she began to wonder whether her father was in fact listening to the woman in the gray dress.

Getting to her feet, she headed quickly to the door, which had creaked shut a few minutes earlier. She didn't know what she was going to do, exactly, but she was filled with the sense that she had to get to her father and make sure that he was alright. She gripped the handle and pulled to open the door, only to swiftly discover that it was locked. That made no sense, of course, since she was not even aware of a key to this particular door; she crouched down and looked through the keyhole, which sure enough was empty. Nevertheless, when she got to her feet and turned the handle again, she found that it was still locked.

"How can this be?" she muttered under her breath, pulling repeatedly on the handle. "It makes no sense."

Indeed, she could determine no reason why this door – which was supposed to open inward, and which quite clearly was not locked in any conventional sense – refused to yield. Yet the more she pulled on the handle, the more she felt the door strengthening its resolve, until she began to worry that the handle itself was going to come loose. She knew she should step back and try to come up with a better strategy, yet she couldn't help turning the handle again and again as she felt a sort of panic fill her chest. And all the while, her father -

Suddenly the door jerked open, and Patience had to step back in order to keep its edge from slamming straight into her face. Letting out a shocked gasp, she found that her father was now standing on the other side, out on the landing.

"What are you doing?" he asked sternly.

"I..."

She hesitated, but in that moment she wondered whether the darkness behind him might be forming some kind of shape, almost as if a shadow was loitering just out of sight. She blinked and the sensation immediately faded.

"I -"

"You were making the most tremendous noise," he continued, before taking a moment to check the handle. "Why, I think you were well on your way to dismantling this door. You might only by a young woman, but you have more strength about you than I had perhaps judged."

"I'm sorry, Father," she told him, trying to regain her composure. "I couldn't get it to open, and I think I juts began to panic."

"I shall examine it later," he replied. "It's getting late and there is much to do tomorrow." He turned and walked toward the top of the stairs. "I want you to go to sleep now, Patience. I need you to be rested for the morning."

"To sleep?" She furrowed her brow. "But Father, what about our guest."

He stopped and turned to her, and she could already see a hint of confusion in his eyes.

“What about our guest?” she asked again. “Does Father Ward not require another drink, perhaps?”

“Who?” Samuel asked, before shaking his head. “Oh, the priest. No, the priest has departed. He said nothing of any great interest. I believe he merely wished to introduce himself, and perhaps to snoop a little, but he has been dealt with. Now prepare for bed, Patience. There is no sense staying up late, not when the morning will bring more work.”

***

A few hours later, as she lay in darkness in her bed, Patience stared at the opposite wall. Moonlight was streaming through the window, casting the shadows of dancing branches across the room. Usually a sight such as this would calm Patience's mind and help her drift away into sleep, but on this occasion her thoughts were racing and she felt more awake than ever.

Something about her father's expression, about the way he'd spoken to her, had left her deeply concerned.

“The priest has departed,” she heard him saying as his words drifted once more through her mind. “He said nothing of any great interest. I believe he merely wished to introduce himself, and perhaps to snoop a little, but he has been dealt with. Now prepare for bed, Patience. There is no sense staying up late, not when the morning will bring more work."

Those words seemed so stiff and awkward now, as if they were devoid of her father's usual personality. Although she knew the idea was preposterous, she couldn't help worrying that in some way her father had been told to speak in such a manner, almost as if somebody had forced him while holding a pistol to the back of his head. She recalled the sense of a shadow over his shoulder, and this too seemed impossible, yet she couldn't shake the sense that the truth remained elusively just out of reach, or that she might be able to determine what was really happening if only she thought a little harder.

A little better.

Feeling the bed shift a little, she realized that someone almost seemed to have sat behind her. And then, to her horror, she felt a cold hand on her shoulder. She flinched, stiffening all over, but she could not quite bring herself to turn and look at the intruder. The door to her room had been shut since she had retired – and it remained shut now, as she could just about see from her position on the bed – yet somehow somebody had entered now and was sitting behind her. As she swallowed hard, Patience couldn't help but think of the woman in the gray dress, and she felt absolutely certain that if she turned to look, she would see that very same woman now.

And yet...

And yet, after a few seconds, she began to consider another possibility. The hand felt dead and lifeless, and so very cold, but she wondered whether it might actually belong to her own mother. At first this idea seemed foolish, yet with each passing second she felt more and more at ease as she imagined her own mother having returned to grant her a little comfort. The hand was not moving, certainly, and it was still colder than any hand she had ever felt, yet she couldn't deny that the merest idea of her mother's return left her feeling hugely grateful and secure. Part of her worried that she was being fooled, and she knew she could look up and check for certain, but finally she felt a rush of relief as all her defenses melted away.

"Thank you, Mother," she whispered, as she felt herself slipping – at long last – into sleep. "I'm so glad you've come back to me. Now I shall be able to sleep in peace."

CHAPTER TWENTY-FOUR

ONE WEEK LATER, VOICES called out across the village as the inhabitants of Cobblefield went about their daily routines.

Outside the public house, a man was swilling muck from the wall, while at the rear of the butcher's shop several carcasses were being chopped up. Two women carried baskets along one of the narrow cobbled roads, and at the iron monger's studio a loud hammering sound was already ringing out. In the yard in front of the barn, meanwhile, Daniel Purkiss was busy chipping clumps of dried mud from some equipment that was to be used later in the day.

Hearing raised voices, Daniel looked up and saw that two men had stopped to speak to one another at the entrance to the yard.

"What are they talking about?"

Turning, he saw that his sister Anne was sitting nearby, watching him from the shade.

"I don't know," he told her, "and it's none of my business anyway. The world would be a pretty sorry place if everybody had their noses in everybody else's business, don't you think?"

"What are you doing?"

"Cleaning some tools that Father needs later."

"What tools?"

"You're too young to understand, but they're for the horses." He paused for a moment. "I have to take them out to Comler's Field shortly, and then I need to do a few things on my way back into the village."

"Can I come with you?"

"No, it'll be much easier if I go alone," he replied. "You'll be fine here, though. Can't you play for a while. Believe me, if I could spend my day with no work, I'd feel mighty pleased with myself. There'll come a time, Anne, when you're a busy grown-up woman and you'll look back on these moments, and you'll wish they could return."

"I don't know about that," she said, furrowing her brow and scrunching her nose as she looked down at the rag-doll in her hands. "I suppose Elizabeth and I can keep ourselves busy, though."

"That's the spirit," Daniel said, as he looked

back down at the mud he'd already scraped clear from the equipment. “I won't be long. There are just a few people I must see on my way home. Although if -”

Before he could finish, he spotted a familiar figure riding past the yard on horseback. Samuel Butler was making his way out of the village, no doubt heading off to the east so that he could continue his work for the elusive Mr. Wallace. That realization gave Daniel a flicker of hope, for he realized that – with her father out of the house – Patience would finally be free to meet again at the bridge.

“I have to go,” he told his sister hurriedly, grabbing the piece of metal and heading toward his own horse. “If you like, when I get back, we can play with your dolls for a short while.”

***

Standing on the arched stone bridge, Daniel looked down into the water and saw a couple of fish swim past. Looking up, he glanced along the paths that led away from the bridge on either side, yet still he saw no sign that he was about to be joined.

A whole week had passed since he'd last seen Patience. He'd known from the start that she wouldn't be able to join him every single day, of course, and he was a patient man, yet he couldn't help but wonder whether something might be wrong. She'd seemed so keen to continue the meetings on the bridge, and he felt sure that she should at least have been able to slip away from the house once over the previous week, especially when her father was most certainly away for the day on business.

Yet now, for the seventh day in a row, there was no sign of her at all.

***

Having dismounted from his horse, Daniel led the animal by its reins, heading along the street as he headed back toward the yard. He knew he shouldn't feel too dispirited, yet he couldn't help but wish that he might see Patience again, at least for a minute or two. He'd even considered riding to Hadlow House to check on her, before reminding himself that he had promised to do no such thing.

Now, as he walked past the steps that led up to the gate of St. Leonard's, he supposed that he would simply have to go to the bridge again the next day. And if Patience had tired of him, or had perhaps found herself another suitor, then that was her choice.

Hearing voices, he saw that several men had gathered at the bottom of the steps, wearing somber funeral attire. Cobblefield was a small, close-knit village where everyone knew the local business, and Daniel had most certainly not heard anything about a death in the community. Slowing his pace, he saw that he recognized several of the men who had gathered, and he couldn't help but wonder exactly what had transpired.

"Good morning," he said to the men as he stopped next to them. "Is there a burial today?"

"Did you hear about the woman who was found in the forest?" Matthew Harper asked.

"I believe I heard mention of something, but not the detail. Was her name finally discovered?"

"It was not," Harper replied, "but she was in no state to be kept above the ground any longer. A decision had to be made, so this morning she was buried." He took a moment to clear his throat. "It was a strange thing, to be sure," he added, "to attend the burial of a woman whose name is unknown to those gathered. Still, we did the best thing we could manage, under the circumstances."

"At least there were a few of us there," Henry Boone muttered. "It doesn't seem right for anyone to be buried without mourners."

"Did Father Ward oversee the service?" Daniel asked. "I know he could not be found recently, and that there was some speculation that he might have suddenly had to visit another parish."

"We are still waiting to hear of Father Ward's whereabouts," Harper told him, before clearing his throat yet again. "There are those who say that the man had some family business elsewhere, but I contend that it is exceedingly unlikely that he would have left without speaking to anyone. First we have this woman found dead and naked near that wretched house, now we have a missing priest. I might be worrying about nothing – indeed, I pray that is the case – but I cannot help thinking that something is amiss."

"Where exactly was this woman found?" Daniel replied.

"Out on the edge of Hadlow House's grounds," Harper said, his voice positively dripping with a sense of distaste. "I know I'm not the only person in this village who feels some discomfort whenever that place is mentioned. There was talk of us going out there together to ask the present occupant what he knows, but the consensus now seems to be that we should leave the matter alone. That doesn't sit well with me, but I suppose I cannot go against such a decision."

"So nobody is trying to identify the poor woman who was buried today in an unmarked grave?" Daniel asked.

"The truth will come out eventually," Harper said firmly. "It always does."

As the gathering began to disperse, Daniel was left standing alone with only his horse for company. After a moment he tied it to a nearby post, and then he made his way up the steps and into the cemetery. A man was busy tending to the recently-filled grave, and as Daniel made his way over he saw that this particular grave had no stone. Evidently with nobody to pay for such a thing, and no name to put on it, the dead woman was simply to be interred and forgotten. That, he knew, was more than was achieved for a lot of people, but as he stared at the churned soil he couldn't help but wonder how this woman had ended up being dumped like rubbish beyond the edge of the village.

"Come to put some flowers down, have you?" Edgar Warner asked, grinning as he patted the soil flat. "Someone might as well leave something for her."

"Does absolutely no-one know who this woman was?" Daniel asked, still struggling a little to believe that such a thing was possible.

"Someone out there surely does," Edgar chuckled, "but unless she's a lady or the wife of someone important, I doubt any fellow'll care enough to come and seek her out. You're young, boy, you still have a lot to learn. Sometimes, this is just the way the world works."

"I'm sure it is," Daniel said under his breath, still staring at the grave as he tried to banish the sense of unease from his chest. "Yet the thought of this matter lingers and I am not satisfied." In that moment, he thought once more of Patience and he realized that her absence from the bridge could no longer be ignored. “I fear, indeed, that something is afoot here that must surely be terribly wrong.”

CHAPTER TWENTY-FIVE

A FEW HOURS LATER, dismounting from his horse at the edge of the clearing that led to Hadlow House, Daniel felt a knot of tension in his stomach.

"You'll wait here," he told the horse, tying him to a post before making his way toward the large iron gate at the front of the house. "I just need to know for certain that -"

Before he could finish, he spotted movement on the other side of the gate, out toward the house itself. As he reached the gate and put his hands on the bars, he was relieved by the sight of Patience emptying some kind of pan of water onto the ground. Although every account of the dead woman had described her as being older, until that moment he had been unable to entirely escape the fear that something might have happened to Patience herself. Now he watched for a moment as she finished emptying the pan, and then – as she turned to go back into the house – he could contain himself no longer.

"Patience!" he called out, waving at her. "Over here!"

She turned to him, but she showed no real reaction; although he hadn't exactly expected her to burst with delight, Daniel had at least hoped that she might be pleased to see him. Instead she simply stared, and after a few seconds he began to wonder whether she even recognized him at all.

"It's me!" he shouted. "It's Daniel!"

After a moment she set the pan down and began to walk toward him. He allowed himself a sigh of relief as he realized that at least nothing seemed to be too wrong, and then he opened the gate and stepped through. Glancing around, he saw no sign of Samuel Butler's horse and he supposed that there was ample time to talk to Patience before there was much risk of her father returning.

"I'm sorry for coming here," he told her as she approached. "I know I said I wouldn't, but I heard some worrying tales in the village and I hadn't seen you for a while, so I had to come and make sure that you're alright."

"Daniel," she said softly, stopping in front of him. "This isn't a good time."

"I do not mean to trouble you," he replied. "Just tell me that all is well with you, and I shall turn around and ride away."

"All is well with me," she said, although her voice sounded strangely monotonous, devoid of her usual character. "Now... please, you must go."

"There is but one more thing," he told her. "Now that I see you are good and well, I turn my thoughts to your mother."

"My mother is dead."

"I know, and your father buried her, I believe?"

"That is correct."

"Might I ask where?" He waited for an answer, but she seemed strangely uninterested in the conversation. "I barely met her, of course," he continued, "but still, I should like to pay my respects."

"Father has taken care of things," she replied, "and that is good enough for me. And as for Mother, she -"

Stopping suddenly, she turned and looked back toward the house. Daniel followed her gaze, and for a moment he thought he saw a faint figure at one of the downstairs windows. This figure faded almost immediately, however, and had been so indistinct that it could easily have been a mere shadow. Still, as he looked at Patience again, Daniel was once again struck by the sense that she was far from her usual self.

"I would like to see you at the bridge again one day," he told her, even though he knew he'd promised not to be so pushy. "Just to talk, if that suits you."

"I can't be sure," she replied, turning to him again and reaching for the gate, as if she intended to close it on him. "We shall see. For now, you must depart."

"Just tell me that you're in no danger," he said, surprising himself a little with his tone. He had not meant to express quite so much concern, yet now he realized that perhaps this fear was justified. "Tell me, Patience," he added, "that I should not worry."

"You should not worry," she said firmly. "I'm absolutely fine here with Father and Mother." She paused for a few seconds. "I mean, with Father. Do not trouble yourself, and do not come to the gate again. If I wish to see you, I know where to find you."

With that she pushed the gate shut, and Daniel had to step back in order to keep from having the metal bars bump against his face. He watched as Patience made sure that the gate was properly secured, and then as she turned and made her way back to the house. Although he was relieved to see that she was physically in good health, he couldn't shake the feeling that something was still very wrong with Patience, and deep down he already knew that he was going to have to find some other way to check on her.

***

Somewhere in the distance, an owl hooted.

Having returned to the village and completed all his duties for the day, Daniel had now made his way back – after sundown – to watch the house. He'd seen Samuel's horse tied to a post as soon as he'd arrived, which meant that Mr. Butler was back from his daily tasks, and a few of the house's lower windows were lit by flickering light from some hearth or another. Now, as Daniel sat in a tree a little way back from Hadlow House's wall, he felt a flicker of concern as he spotted Patience working in the kitchen.

She was beautiful, he had to admit that, and the merest sight of her face was enough to bring joy to his heart. Although he hadn't quite admitted as much to himself yet, he was already fond of her in a manner that he had never experienced before; certainly there was no other girl who could have inadvertently led him to mount a late-night vigil. All he knew was that he desperately wanted to see that she was alright, and that – above all – he wanted to be proved a fool.

Eventually Patience disappeared from view. Daniel waited for her to reappear, but as the minutes passed he realized that she might well be on the house's other side. He climbed down from the tree and considered his options, before finally realizing that he had to do the one thing that he'd previously refused to consider. Making his way to the gate, he stopped to check that nobody was watching and then he eased the gate open, slipping into the garden and then hurrying toward the house.

Once he reached the nearest wall, he stopped to listen for any hint that he might have been spotted. Finally he began to creep along one side of the house until he looked through one of the windows, but all he saw so far was what he believed to be the front room or perhaps the reception area. He waited, and then he crept around the corner and made his way to the second window along, which allowed him to look into the dining room. Here he saw only the large, empty table, with no sign of life at all, so he hurried to the far end of the house's side and looked into the kitchen.

Patience was standing at one of the counters, staring straight ahead. Daniel's first thought was to call out to her, but he already knew that she would most likely simply send him away. Besides, he didn't want to get her into trouble by alerting her father, so instead he made his way back the way he'd just came.

Reaching the front of the house, he tried to come up with another plan. No matter how hard, he tried to tell himself that he was imagining things, he was unable to shake a deep sense of concern. He walked quietly past the front door, and as he approached the window looking into the study he realized that he could hear a man's voice speaking softly. He slowed his pace a little, and then he forced himself to be brave; looking into the room, he was surprised to see Samuel Butler kneeling on the floor, facing the far corner. The room was entirely dark, save for a patch of moonlight, but Daniel was just about able to see that the door to the rest of the house was shut.

Why, he wondered, was Samuel Butler kneeling along in one of the rooms?

After pondering that question for a few seconds, Daniel crept around the corner and made his way to the next window. Looking through, he once again saw Mr. Butler on his knees, but he could just about hear the man speaking again. Confused, Daniel had no idea why the man might be speaking at all, but he knew for certain that Patience would not be able to hear from her position all the way over in the kitchen. Watching Mr. Butler for a moment, he began to wonder whether the man might be praying, although something about his tone of voice suggested otherwise.

And then, as he continued to watch, Daniel began to realize that Mr. Butler was kneeling before an old chair that had been placed in the corner of the room. This was strange enough, but a few seconds later Daniel's eyes adjusted even more and he found himself wondering whether there might perhaps be some kind of shape in the chair, a shadow or perhaps even a human figure.

Leaning closer to the glass, he held his breath as he tried to make out this figure. He hoped that he would quickly see that there was nobody at all, yet if anything the figure was becoming more and more distinct with each passing second, until finally it seemed to lean forward a little, revealing the angry face of a woman. A moment later, before Daniel could react, this woman screamed.

CHAPTER TWENTY-SIX

STUMBLING BACK, DANIEL TRIPPED on a rough patch of dirt and fell to the ground. Shocked to his core, he stared up at the window as the scream faded to nothing, but already he knew that he had recognized the sound.

He'd heard the exact same scream before, when he was out on the road with Patience.

Stumbling to his feet, he instinctively took a couple of steps toward the window, before holding back. Already he could see that Samuel Butler was still on his knees, but he was surprised to notice that the man had not reacted at all to the scream, as if he hadn't even heard it ringing out. Wondering how such a thing might be possible, Daniel hesitated for a few seconds before hurrying to the farthest window, and when he looked into the kitchen he saw that Patience was calmly washing some dishes, as if she too was oblivious to the sound that had just shaken the entire house.

"How is this possible?" Daniel whispered.

Taking a moment to try to come up with an idea, he knew that he couldn't simply turn around and leave the house as if nothing had happened. He thought of the fury on the face of the woman he'd just seen, and he knew that this was most certainly not Patience's mother. A few seconds later, spotting a gap in one of the other windows, he made his way over and found that it had been left slightly open. After fiddling for a moment with the latch, he pulled the window open all the way and peered into the darkness, and as his eyes adjusted to the gloom he realized that he had found a way to get into some kind of storage room.

He briefly considered knocking on the front door, and then – realizing that he needed to take more direct action – he climbed through the window and dropped down into the darkened room on the other side.

After a few seconds of stillness, he realized that he had not been heard. Still, as his eyes adjusted and he crept across the room, he realized that the only exit led into the study, which meant that he could not escape the room without going directly past Mr. Butler and the ghostly woman in the chair. He stared at the door for a moment, wondering if he dared to make such a move, and then – as he took another step forward – his right foot bumped against something on the floor. Looking down, he expected to see a box or a bag of some kind, but as his eyes became more accustomed to the darkness he was just about able to make out the slumped form of a man.

Crouching down, he rolled the man onto his back and saw a pair of dead eyes staring up toward the ceiling. He leaned a little closer, and now he was starting to recognize this man.

"Father Ward?" he whispered, as he saw that the priest's neck was horribly twisted and contorted, in a manner that was by no means conducive to life.

Horrified, he leaned back and tried to work out exactly what he should do next. A fraction of a second later, however, he heard footsteps approaching the door; he pulled back behind a set of shelves just in time, for the door swiftly open and the unmistakable silhouette of Samuel Butler filled the opening.

"Yes," Samuel said after a moment, "I know you're right. He can't be kept here for too much longer."

He paused, before turning and looking out into the study.

"I shall do it while Patience is busy," he continued. "It would be as well for the girl to know nothing of this, lest she might make a scene."

As he pulled back further into the dark corner, Daniel watched with a growing sense of horror as Samuel picked the dead priest up and slung him over his shoulder. Then, turning and walking out, Samuel seemed to struggle a little with the weight, and in the process a heavy book fell from the dead man's pockets.

"I shall not be long," he announced. "I shall leave him where I left Rose."

The door began to swing shut, just as Daniel heard another door clicking open. He could also hear Patience still working in the kitchen, so he was not overly surprised when she seemingly did not notice her father opening the front door and stepping out of the house. The door bumped shut again, and after a few seconds Daniel was left hearing only the noise of Patience still working hard.

Although he knew he had to get to the kitchen as swiftly as possible, Daniel still hesitated for a few seconds. He thought back to the sight of the dead woman in the chair, and he knew that the chair was waiting just beyond the door that he saw now. Although he had always considered himself to be a brave man, he still had to summon the courage to take even the slightest step forward, and already he could feel a knot of dread tightening in his chest. Every thought in his head was screaming at him to turn around and run, but he kept thinking of

Patience working quietly and obediently in the kitchen.

With Samuel out of the house, Patience was at the mercy of the ghostly woman. He saw the priest's Bible on the floor, and in that moment he understood that he had to do the right thing.

Once he was in the study, Daniel stopped and looked around. He knew that the ghost could be hiding, and that it might appear at any moment, but so far there was no sign of it at all. Once he was sure that the chair in the corner looked entirely empty, he made his way across the room and pulled the door open. He looked out into the hallway, and immediately he realized that he could just about make out the sound of Patience speaking to someone.

"Dear Lord," he whispered under his breath, "protect us from..."

His voice trailed off for a moment as he realized that he was not entirely sure how to finish that sentence. The woman in the chair seemed so far removed from anything holy that he worried even God would not be able to help.

"I know," Patience was saying up ahead, as Daniel made his way slowly across the hallway, passing the foot of the staircase, "Father works so very hard and I must support him. Of late, I have tried so hard to make the house a restful place, but I know I still have much to learn. That is why I am so grateful to you for returning like this. Without you, Mother, I do not know what I would do."

Reaching the doorway, Daniel looked through and saw that Patience was still working at the counter, drying some plates. There was seemingly nobody else in the room, yet as he glanced around Daniel felt certain that there must be another presence nearby.

"Oh, but you're so right," Patience continued suddenly, as if she had heard some remark in the silence.

Daniel looked at her again, and he was quite sure now that his own arrival had gone unnoticed.

"Father deserves only the very best," Patience said with a faint smile. "I never appreciated how much work you did, Mother. I suppose I was just a foolish girl, and I believed that the household more or less ran itself. Now I see the truth, however, and I understand that you were working miracles."

Daniel took another step forward, and in that moment he inadvertently bumped the side of a pan that was resting on a nearby bench.

Patience immediately turned to him.

"Daniel," she said, clearly shocked, "what are you doing here? I didn't hear you come in. Father might see you!"

"Your father has left the house," he said cautiously. "Did you not hear?"

"I must have been in a world of my own," she told him. "Still, you really shouldn't be here when he gets back. If he -"

"Didn't you hear the scream?" he asked.

"I beg your pardon?"

"Can it not be heard from within the house?" he continued. "Patience, not ten minutes ago, a scream rang out that must have easily been heard from the road."

"You are quite mistaken," she replied. "Daniel, I have not moved from this spot in all that time and more, and I would most certainly have heard a scream if one had -"

Stopping suddenly, she turned to her left, as if she had once again heard a silent voice.

"What's that?" she whispered, before nodding gently. "You're quite right. Of course. I'm sorry, Mother, I should not indulge such foolishness."

She turned to Daniel again.

"You must -"

"That is *not* your mother," Daniel said firmly, interrupting her as he began to make out the faintest hint of a dark shape behind Patience. "I have seen its face and it is something else entirely."

"Daniel, you're troubling me," Patience replied. "Please, you must leave, for Father will most certainly be back soon."

"I'm not leaving without you," he told her,

as the figure over her shoulder became clearer still. Already, the gray dress was just about visible. "Patience," he added, holding out his right hand, "I need you to come with me immediately."

"I cannot do that," she told him. "Surely you must understand, Daniel, that I have to focus on my work for Father. Speaking of which, you are preventing me from doing that work, so please -"

"Patience, we're leaving!" he snapped as he began to see the angry, snarling face of the dead woman once more. He stepped forward and tried to grab her hand. "Patience, you must see the truth. If you think this thing is your mother, you are wrong."

"Mother has come back to help me," she replied, and now her smile was growing. "She knows best, and she's teaching me how to look after Father. Daniel, your concern is touching but it is also misplaced. Please, leave me to get on with my tasks."

"Patience -"

Suddenly the ghostly figure screamed again, lunging at Daniel and this time grabbing him by the throat. Before he could even try to pull away, he was sent crashing past the counter until he slammed into the wall, and he could only manage a pained gasp as the dead woman squeezed his throat tight and leaned closer until she was screaming directly into his face.

CHAPTER TWENTY-SEVEN

"MOTHER, WHAT ARE YOU doing?" Patience gasped, horrified by the sight of Daniel struggling and pinned to the wall. She took a step forward. "Mother, if -"

In that moment the woman turned and snarled at her, and Patience stopped in her tracks as she realized that something was terribly wrong.

"Wait ," she stammered, as Daniel continued to try to pull away, "you're not Mother!"

Letting go of Daniel, leaving him to slump down to the floor, the spectral woman turned to Patience and began to make her way back across the kitchen.

"You're tired," she sneered, "and there is still much you do not understand about this world. My dear, return to your task and make sure that it is done to perfection. I shall rid the house of this intruder, so that you no longer have to worry."

Patience immediately turned to do as she was told, but at the last second she held back. Trembling with fear, she felt an urge to obey, yet after a few seconds she turned to the woman again and realized that she looked nothing like her mother at all; indeed, she now wondered how she could ever have been so mistaken.

"Who are you?" she asked. "What -"

"Idiot!" the woman screamed, grabbing her by the shoulder and throwing her across the room, sending her slamming into the wall.

Falling down, Patience let out a gasp of pain. She tried to get up, but a sharp burst of agony rippled through her side and she found that she was unable to get to her feet at all.

"You shall have to learn your lesson again," the ghostly figured said, as Patience managed to turn and look up at her. "I had thought you might be more willing to learn your role, yet evidently you have need of a harsher form of discipline. Fortunately you have me as a teacher, and I was once the greatest housekeeper any man could ask for." She stopped and leaned down toward Patience, who was now shaking frantically with fear. "I might not have been able to serve Mr. Hadlow as I had wished," the woman continued, "but I shall not let this second chance pass me by."

"Please," Patience sobbed, "why are you so angry?"

"I merely mean to make you work properly," the woman continued. "You understand that, my dear, do you not?"

"Yes," Patience said, too scared to think otherwise. "Mother, is that you? Mother, if -"

"Move!"

Suddenly Daniel grabbed her by the arm and pulled her out of the way, forcing her along the corridor until they reached the hallway.

"That woman is not your mother!" he hissed. "I don't know what hold she has over you and your father, but evidently she is some demon sent to torture you both."

"It's my mother," she said, stopping and turning to him. "Daniel, you must understand, I -"

Before she could get another word out, however, she spotted a figure sitting in the dining room. Shocked, she stared past Daniel and saw that another woman – wearing a dark dress this time – was sitting hunch on the other side of the dining table, seemingly sobbing violently as she faced the window with her head in her hands. Patience opened her mouth to call out, but in that moment she realized that she had never seen this woman before in her life.

"Patience?" Daniel asked, before turning to follow her gaze. He immediately saw the woman too. “It is another apparition,” he continued. “It must be.”

“She is upset,” Patience replied, stepping past him. “I must go to her.”

“It is another specter of the dead!” Daniel snapped angrily. He looked toward the kitchen; the other ghost was nowhere to be seen, but the one in the dining room was crying now with greater and greater volume. “Patience, we must be out of this house so that you can clear your head and think properly!”

“Who are you?” Patience asked, stepping into the dining room as she kept her gaze fixed on the woman's sobbing, heaving shoulders. “Pray tell me, for I have seen you not before. Why are you here, in my father's house?”

The woman continued to sob, and as Patience edged closer she realized that she could see something dark and wet glistening in the woman's hair. Approaching from behind, Patience furrowed her brow as she tried to work out exactly what she was witnessing, and then she let out a horrified cry as she saw the truth: the back of the woman's head had been damaged by some kind of heavy blow, breaking the skin and cracking the skull, and now maggots or something other foul creatures were infesting the wound. For a few seconds, Patience could only watch the hideous, fat monstrosities as they squirreled and squirmed their way through sections of exposed brain.

"Have you seen him?" the woman gasped, sitting up but still not turning to look at Patience. "Tell me, it has been so long, but have you seen my dear Richard?"

"I don't know who you're talking about," Patience replied cautiously.

"We must go!" Daniel hissed from the doorway. "Patience, there is no time for this!"

"Has she driven him away forever?" the woman whimpered. "I feared as much, yet my heart tells me that it cannot be true. He would not leave me here to suffer at her hand."

She began to turn, before pausing for a moment.

"Or would he?"

"I don't know what you mean," Patience said, even as she felt Daniel pulling on her hand and trying to get her to leave the room. "Please, can't you tell me who you are?"

"Perhaps I disappointed him," the woman cried, turning a little more until finally she was facing Patience, revealing her dark and rotten eyes. "Perhaps I was not the wife he wanted." She began to get to her feet. "Perhaps Fanny is right to keep me here and torture me so."

"Fanny?" Patience asked. "Who's Fanny?"

"Run!" the woman screamed suddenly, her voice screeching through the air that she even caused the windowpanes to rattle in their frames. “Run before it is too late! Don't let her get you! You must run!”

Stumbling back out into the hallway, Patience stared in horror at the woman until – a moment later – the dining room door slammed shut with such force that it rattled loudly.

“Who was that?” Patience asked, turning to Daniel. “What -”

In that moment, she saw a figure silhouetted in the doorway that led to the kitchen. She stared for a moment, wondering whether her mother had returned once more, but somehow the other woman's voice was ringing in her head and reminding her that her greatest hope was going to be dashed.

“That is not your mother,” Daniel said firmly, having also spotted the woman. He squeezed Patience's hand tighter still. “Please, you must see that we need to leave this place.”

“Then who else can it be?” Patience asked, as tears once again began to fill her eyes. “Surely you must be mistaken, for no-one else could be in -”

She stopped suddenly, as soon as the figure in the doorway stepped forward and her pale, dead features were revealed. Something about the woman's face immediately struck fear into Patience's eyes, and although she had been about to step forward, now she was filled with a sense of utter revulsion. Somehow, deep down, she knew now that the woman she saw was abhorrent, and counter to any received notion of nature.

"Who is she?" she stammered. "Daniel, who is that woman and what is she doing in my home?"

"We can try to answer that question later," he replied, taking her by the hand and leading her toward the front door. "There will be time once we are out of this house, but I fear that while we are within these walls we are in danger of falling under her spell."

He grabbed the handle and pulled the door open.

"If we are to have clear heads -"

Before he could finish, he let out a shocked gasp as he almost slammed straight into Samuel Butler. Standing firmly on the door's other side, with his large frame almost entirely filling the space, Patience's father glared into the house with a dark stare for a few seconds, before slowly turning to Patience.

"Father," she said, her voice tense with fear, "we are in danger if we stay here. I do not know who she is, but our home has been invaded by some entity."

"That is no entity," Samuel said, pushing her back and stepping into the hallway, before shoving the door shut. "I had hoped that you would be better behaved, Patience. Now it is evident to me that you need to face the highest form of discipline."

CHAPTER TWENTY-EIGHT

"IN HERE!"

Pulling on Patience's hand, Daniel led her into the next room, which happened to be the study. Shutting the door before Samuel could follow, he quickly pushed a chair under the handle in a makeshift attempt to keep Patience's father out, and then he took a step back.

"Open this door at once!" Samuel called out, trying the handle, only for the chair to do its job admirably. "Patience, do you hear me? I will not be denied entry into a room in my own house!"

He tried the handle again, rattling the door, as Daniel and Patience both took a step back.

"What's wrong with him?" she asked. "I hope that I am mistaken, but I cannot shake the feeling that my father is somehow... not my father."

"You were right," Daniel replied, turning to her. "There *is* a foul spirit in this house, and it seems to have cast its spell over your father. Until a few minutes ago, it had done the same to you."

"I do not recall any such thing," she told him.

"I'm not surprised, but you were talking to her in the kitchen as if she was your mother."

"I remember now," she muttered, furrowing her brow as Samuel tried yet again to get the door open. "At least, I think I do. It's like a dream, but I think I was standing in the kitchen and my mother had come to help me."

"That was not your mother," Daniel told her. "It was the spirit, whoever and whatever she might be."

"The ghostly woman in the dining room mentioned someone named Fanny," she pointed out. "Who could that be?"

"There is a Frances Baxter buried in the local cemetery," he explained, "and I believe she worked here at the house. If she was one of the servants murdered by Mr. Hadlow, it's entirely possible that her spirit lingers here and seeks to gain some satisfaction for her death. We have no way of knowing exactly what she's after, Patience, but I'm quite sure that she exerts her influence only within the house itself. You heard her scream when we were on the road, but not when you were inside."

"My father seems drawn to her."

"Your father -"

Daniel hesitated for a moment, wondering how much to tell her, but he quickly realized that she needed to know everything.

"Your father, I fear, is involved in the death of the local priest."

"Father Ward?" She paused, before shaking her head. "No, he came to visit some time ago, but he left."

"His body was in the room over there," Daniel replied, leading her to the doorway in the corner and then pointing at the floor, where the dead man's Bible still lay. "Your father took him out into the forest this very evening, no doubt to abandon his corpse in the same spot as your mother's poor body."

"He buried my mother," she replied uncertainly.

"I'm sorry to tell you this," he said, as Samuel yet again tried to open the door, "but your mother's earthly remains were discovered last week by two poachers."

"No," she said, shaking her head, and now tears were streaming down her face. "Why are you saying such things? Father told me that he gave her a proper burial."

"Did you see the plot?"

"No, but only because..."

Her voice trailed off as she began to realize the awful truth.

"Patience!" Samuel shouted, hitting the door with force now. "What are you doing in there? I demand that you open this door at once!"

"The window is open," Daniel said, lowering his voice a little. "Patience, I cannot claim that I know everything we should do here tonight, but it is clear to me that you and your father have been put in danger by this spirit. Come with me, we can get out through the window and then we shall think of some way to help your father."

"I cannot leave him," she replied.

"It is only temporary," he told her. "We shall come back to save him, I promise, but I cannot risk letting that creature get into your mind again. Patience, if the ghost wanted to harm your father, she could easily have done so by now. The fact that she has let you both live means that she has some other desire, but right now I need to get you away from here before she traps you again."

"Patience!" Samuel shouted, banging his fists against the door. "You will come out at once!"

"We can take soundings," Daniel continued, "from those who are better placed to know how we can deal with such a situation. We cannot be expected to devise a solution ourselves, but at least if we get away, you and I can come up with some way to help your father." He squeezed her hand. "I will not leave you here alone with that woman, Patience."

"I know you won't," she told him, before stepping toward the storage room's open window. "I can only pray that you are right."

"We are ill-equipped to know how to handle the dead," he pointed out as he gestured for her to climb through the window first. "Father Ward is dead, but there must be someone we can contact who will know how to deal with this situation."

"You must go first," she replied. "Hurry!"

"But -"

"Hurry, Daniel!" she hissed, pushing him toward the window. "There is no time to argue, and I have more need of your assistance to get down than to get up!"

Reasoning that she had a good point, Daniel quickly climbed out through the window. Dropping onto the ground, he reached out to help Patience through, only for her to slam the window shut and immediately slide the latch into place.

"What are you doing?" he shouted.

"I'm sorry," she replied, raising her voice so that she could be heard, "but I'm not leaving my father at the mercy of that woman. I am sure that she will not hurt me, at least not initially, but I cannot be so sure about you." She took a moment to adjust the latch. "You can break the glass if you want, Daniel, but I am sure you will not be able to break the wood itself and climb back inside. Even if you do, the process will take too long." She took a step back. "You must trust me. I even believe that I have an idea."

With that, she turned and walked away.

"Let me in!" he shouted, slamming his fist on the window. "Patience, I won't let you do this! You can't face her alone!"

Stopping on the other side of the room, Patience reached down and picked up Father Ward's Bible.

"She seems to have been very keen to kill the priest," she said firmly, as she tried to work out *exactly* how her plan was going to proceed. "That suggests to me that she feared him in some way. Mother's Bible is upstairs, so this one will have to do." She looked at the tattered book and told herself that surely it had to be enough. "This entity can't be so strong, not if it fears us. That must mean that we can yet find a way to drive her out."

"Patience, don't do this!" Daniel yelled from the other side of the window. "I'll break in if I have to!"

"You won't have time," she replied, stepping through into the study and then hurrying to the door, where she stopped as she heard her father continuing to batter the other side. "Lord, deliver us from evil," she whispered, as she continued to clutch the Bible, "and let us escape this woman's wrath. We have always tried to do the right thing, and I can only pray that you see us on this night and recognize that we are dealing with something that is most unnatural."

"Open this door!" Samuel shouted angrily. "No daughter of mine is going to act in this disgraceful manner!"

"Give me the strength that I need," Patience whispered, clutching the Bible tighter than ever, "and help me save my father from this evil."

She hesitated for a few more seconds, before pulling the chair away and opening the door.

"Father," she said breathlessly, "I -"

Before she could finish, he slapped her hard on the side of the face, knocking her down onto the floor. The Bible fell from her hands and slid over to the wall, and a moment later – as she tried to get up – Patience felt her father grab her hair tight from behind and pull her head back. Shocked, she looked up and saw him glaring down at her with the ghostly woman standing just a few feet further away.

"You have brought shame and dishonor upon our family," Samuel sneered, tightening his grip on her hair. "I cannot let that go unpunished!"

CHAPTER TWENTY-NINE

"THAT'S NOT MOTHER!" PATIENCE screamed as she saw the hatred on the woman's face. "Father, you have to realize that something else is in our home!"

"Quieten your tongue," he replied, turning and stepping out of the room, dragging her by the hair into the hallway. "Every word you say now will only make your punishment worse!"

"You have to listen to me!" she shouted, trying to pull free even as she was pulled kicking and struggling toward the kitchen. "Father, I'm telling the truth!"

As she was dragged past the door to the dining room, she looked up and saw the ghostly figure in the dark dress, the same woman who had warned her earlier.

"I told you," the woman said mournfully, before stepping back into the darkness. "You should have got away from Fanny while you still had the chance."

"Help me!" Patience shouted, trying to reach out to the woman even though she was already gone. "Who are you? Please, you have to help me!"

Before she could get another word out, Samuel threw her to the floor. Letting out a pained cry, she slammed against the wood and immediately began to get up, before hesitating as she realized that her father was standing over her. On her knees now, she looked up and saw his stony, disapproving face glaring back down at her, and she realized to her horror that for the first time in her life she was truly terrified of the man. Until that moment she had always seen her father as a strong, reliable and most importantly *good* man; now she trembled to think of what he might do if she disobeyed him again.

"Father," she stammered, her voice shaking with fear, "I know it's not my place to question you, but I beg to say..."

Swallowing hard, she felt a tear run down her cheek. A moment later she felt something bump hard against her back, almost knocking her over; she turned and saw a shadowy figure moving past, wearing a gray dress and quickly disappearing into the shadows.

"Father," Patience continued, "I beg you to see what is happening here. That spirit, whatever it is, is not Mother."

She watched the darkness at the far end of the kitchen, terrified in case the figure returned, and then she looked up at her father again. He hadn't moved, he hadn't given any indication whatsoever that her words were getting through to him, but she felt sure that she might still be able to get through to him.

"Father," she said again, crawling forward and reaching up to take his hand, "you must -"

Suddenly he struck her across the face with his other hand, bringing a cry from her lips as she fell back and slumped once again onto the floor. At the same moment, she heard a series of heavy thuds against the front door, as if Daniel was trying to break his way into the house.

"You speak of things you do not understand," he said darkly. "You, a mere child, dare to tell me what I should be doing. What I should be thinking. This is my house, Patience, or have you forgotten that? And while I am the master of this place, you *will* obey me. You might not agree with my decisions, but I am under no obligation to explain them to you. Is that clear?"

"Father -"

"Is that clear?" he roared, stepping toward her.

Instinctively pulling away, Patience let out a terrified cry as she scurried into the corner. She held her hands up to protect her face, and then she saw to her relief that her father was no closer.

"Are you scared of me?" he asked incredulously.

"Father, please," she sobbed, "there is something about this house that does us no good. I think once we are out of it, we can think properly. We just have to get away from -"

In that moment she spotted the shadowy figure again, moving behind her father as if to remind him of her presence. Unable to quite make out the figure's features, Patience nevertheless felt sure that this was the same ghostly woman she had spied on several occasions, the one who had attempted to pass as her dead mother. Pulling herself up, she tried to work out how to make her father see sense, but she worried that he was now entirely under the influence of the malevolent spirit.

Meanwhile, Daniel was still pounding on the front door.

"You have duties still to perform tonight," Samuel said, stepping forward and reaching a hand down toward his daughter. "Before you retire to bed, you must make the kitchen clean. You understand that, do you not?"

She opened her mouth to beg again for him to see the truth, but she knew that to do so would only mean inviting more violence. After a few seconds, therefore, she took his hand and allowed him to help her all the way up, and then she turned and saw the various unclean pots on the counter. She hated the idea of simply returning to her domestic duties, but deep down she was starting to wonder whether this might in fact be her best option; after all, she might yet come up with another way to reason with her father, but she would need time first in which to come up with such a plan.

Finally, slowly, she stepped forward.

"Of course," she said, still unable to hide the fear from her voice as she approached the pans and picked one up. "I shall make you proud, Father."

She began to scrub the pan, but a moment later she felt a cold, dead hand on her shoulder. She knew this was not her father, that this was instead the woman who tormented the house, but after a few seconds she felt a flicker of calmness trickling through her body. Was it not possible, she realized now, that the strange spirit meant only to serve and help the family? Was it not possible that this woman had been misunderstood for so long, and that there was no harm at all in acquiescing to her demands?

"I shall do as I am told," Patience whimpered, with tears still running down her cheeks as she turned the pot around and scrubbed its other side. She flinched at the continued touch of the dead woman, and when she looked at the dark window straight ahead she saw not only her own reflection but also the stern face of the figure directly over her shoulder.

Somehow, she managed not to scream.

"I shall *always* do exactly as I am told," she continued, and now her bottom lip was trembling with terror. "I shall never question you again, Father."

As Daniel continued to hammer the door, Patience sensed her father stepping to her side. She flinched again, but this time she managed to stay on her feet as she focused her attention onto the pot. One particularly stubborn piece of grit was simply refusing to budge from the metal side.

"This is all I have ever wanted, Patience," Samuel said softly, touching her arm. "My -"

"No!" she gasped, pulling away and raising the pot, terrified that he was about to strike her again.

"Do you fear me so much?" he asked, his voice betraying a sense of doubt. "My own daughter cowers from me as if she thinks me a common criminal. Patience, it breaks my heart to see -"

Suddenly they both heard a crashing sound, followed by footsteps, and they turned just in time to see Daniel racing into the room.

"Patience!" he shouted, racing toward her. "Are you alright?"

She hesitated, before doing something that –

in any other circumstance – would have filled her with horror. Looking at her father, she saw the confusion on his face, and then she swung the pot with such force that she knocked him out cold and sent him crumpling down onto the floor.

"Patience?" Daniel said, stopping and looking down at Samuel for a moment, before turning to her again. "Are you -"

"We have to get him out of here," she stammered, throwing the pot aside and grabbing one of Samuel's arms, before gesturing for Daniel to take the other. "There's no time to debate the matter. Once he's out of the house and away from her influence, I'm quite sure I can make him see reason, but we have to hurry!"

Taking Samuel's right arm, Daniel began to help her drag him out of the kitchen and through to the hallway.

"She's close," Patience said, glancing around in case there was any sign of the ghostly figure. "I think she's not always as strong as she'd like to be. I'm quite sure that her influence ends once we're outside the door."

"I hope you're right," he replied, as they managed to pull Samuel out through the door and into the cold night air. "I don't mind admitting that there's much about this night that I shall need explained to me."

"I shall do my best," she told him, "but -"

At that moment, Samuel's body caught on something in the doorway. Looking back up, Patience saw that one leg of his trousers had snagged on a nail just inside the house. Realizing that there was still precious little time to waste, she stepped over her father and made her way back inside, and then she reached down and – after a little jiggling – managed to unhook the fabric.

"Okay," she said, looking at Daniel again, "I think -"

In that moment, she saw the utter horror in his eyes and she realized that something must be behind her. Before she could react, she was pulled back and sent slamming into the wall, before the front door slammed shut and the ghostly woman in the gray dress appeared in the gloom.

"Very well," the woman snarled icily. "If I cannot have him, then I shall just have to make do with you!"

CHAPTER THIRTY

AS PATIENCE STARED UP at the woman, she heard Daniel trying once more to get the front door open. Some hidden force was stopping him, however, and after a few seconds the ghostly woman stepped forward.

"I gave my life," the woman sneered, "in service of Mr. Hadlow and his wives, and how was I repaid? I did everything in my power to save Mr. Hadlow from the horror of his first wife's death, yet he did nothing to protect me when she returned from the grave. She mistook my actions for cruelty, when in fact they were pity!"

"I don't know what you're talking about," Patience stammered, looking around as she tried to find some way to escape. "Please, I just want to get out of here."

"They all abandoned me, in the end," the woman continued. "Oliver left, although he was never much use. The Hadlows are gone, save for that sniveling wretch in the dining room. The sound of her weakness haunts my every moment."

Turning to look into the study, Patience spotted a book resting on the floor. She immediately realized that this was the Bible that she'd dropped earlier, the one that had belonged to Father Ward. She hesitated, and she knew that although this book might yet save her, she had but one chance to get it into her hands.

"My name," the ghostly woman said darkly, "is Fanny Baxter, and I will have my revenge, even if it must be after I am dead."

"I suppose that's understandable," Patience whispered, before looking up at her again. She realized now that she had to cause a distraction. "So you've been dead for a while, I take it. Have you been just haunting this house for all these years? Are you not lonesome?"

"Why would you care about such things?" Fanny asked. "What -"

Suddenly scrambling to her feet, Patience ran into the study and grabbed the Bible. She briefly considered shutting the door and trying to hide, but she could hear Daniel once again trying to break down the door and she understood in that moment that she had to be brave. After all, if all the doors and windows were sealed by the malevolent spirit, there was no point hiding forever.

A fraction of a second later, she heard a floorboard creaking at the foot of the stairs.

"No!" Patience shouted, turning and holding the Bible up, then stepping out into the hallway. Keeping the book aimed at Fanny's face, she tried to keep her hands from shaking. "You must fear this! It's a mark of everything godly and true, of everything pure, of everything you are not!"

She waited, and for a few seconds Fanny stared at the book. After a few seconds, however, the dead woman reached out and took hold of the Bible, and she slowly pulled it from Patience's hands.

"This is strange," Fanny mused, staring down at the book. "Where once a simple cross was enough to drive me away, now this book does nothing." She paused, before a smile began to spread across her lips. "I am perhaps becoming stronger," she whispered. "Or, quite possibly, I am becoming less fearful."

She strengthened her grip, and in that moment the book began to blacken. Staring in horror, Patience stepped back and watched as the Bible turned to dust and ash, finally crumbling between Fanny's fingers and falling to the floor.

"Now look at that," Fanny sneered, turning to Patience again. "I have strengths of which I was not aware. I think I am going to enjoy testing those out!"

With that she lunged at Patience, who ducked out of the way just in time and stumbled into the front room. Turning, she slammed the door shut and then took a few steps back, before rushing to the window and trying to get it open. A moment later she saw Daniel on the other side, slamming his fists against the glass, but there seemed to be no way to break into or out of the house.

"Patience!" he shouted. "Nothing works!"

"She's sealing it somehow," she replied, "and -"

In that moment she heard the door ripping open, pulling away from its hinges, and she turned just in time to see it fall down. Fanny was out in the hallway, glaring through at her with a furious smile that seemed filled simultaneously with both anger and pleasure.

"I'm going to enjoy this," Fanny told her. "I have spent these past decades fearful of godly things, yet now it seems I have no reason to fear anything at all!"

"I have to get out of here," Patience stammered, looking around the room before spotting the old fireplace. She hesitated, and in that moment she realized that she might yet have one last option. "Damn it," she said under her breath," not again."

Racing across the room, she clambered into the fireplace and looked up. She could see nothing but darkness, but she heard the sound of the wind whistling high above and she reasoned that this might yet be one way out of the house that had not been sealed. Wasting no more time, she began to climb, using every ounce of her remaining strength and utilizing all the little tricks she'd learned as a child cleaning chimneys in London. She winced and struggled a little, and her progress was slow, but gradually she began to make her way up and when she looked back down she saw no sign that Fanny was able to follow.

Struggling for breath, she reached up and began to haul herself higher, scrambling past the bricks. She began to cough as thick soot filled her lungs, yet sheer terror was somehow driving her onward. Soon she was at least halfway up, and she began to believe the impossible, that she had finally found a way out of the house. And then, reaching up again, her left hand felt a gap in the bricks and she froze as she remembered her previous time in this chimney.

The gap opened into the main bedroom upstairs, and there would once again be nothing to stop Fanny reaching through.

For a moment, frozen in terror, she felt that she could go no higher. Finally, however, she realized that she had no choice, that the alternative was to either climb back down and face the dead woman again or spend the rest of her life trapped in a chimney. She could hear Daniel still pounding on the door downstairs, and after a moment she took as deep a breath as she dared and then she began to climb again, determined to this time keep going and not let anything stop her.

Suddenly a hand burst through the gap, grabbing her by the throat and slamming her head against the chimney's bricks. Panicking, Patience pushed back but she quickly found that she was already too late.

"You are going nowhere!" Fanny shrieked angrily as Patience struggled to break free. "I will not be left alone in this house again!"

"Leave me alone!" Patience gasped, still fighting frantically even though she knew the dead woman's grip was far too strong. "I want nothing to do with this house ever again! I rue the day my family set foot in the place!"

"Then you must learn to see differently," Fanny said, tightening her grip still further. "If you refuse to stay while alive, then perhaps I shall have to take measures to trap you here. As the dead are trapped!"

Unable to breathe at all, Patience felt herself starting to slip. She looked up and – in the gloom – she was just about able to make out a square patch of starry sky high above, but that patch might as well have been a million miles away. She was so close to escaping, but as tears filled her eyes she knew that at any moment she was about to lose her grip. Refusing to submit so easily, she resolved to fight for as long as possible even as she felt Fanny's sharp fingernails starting to slice into her throat. She knew that only seconds remained, and finally she felt her purchase starting to fail.

"Run!" another voice shouted suddenly. "Patience, leave this place!"

Startled, she felt Fanny's grip loosen. Looking down, she saw that a second hand had now also reached through the gap and was prising Fanny's fingers away. Pulling back, she realized she was free.

"Patience go!" her mother's voice called out desperately from the hold in the chimney's wall. "I can't hold her back forever, but you have to leave while you still can!"

Scrambling further up, Patience felt as if she might yet fall at any moment. Somehow she managed to keep going, however, and finally she did something she had never done before in all her life. She had climbed many chimneys as a child, of course, but she had always ended up shimmying back down; now, for the first time ever, she hauled herself up and out through the top, stumbling onto the roof of Hadlow House and then stopping to get her balance back as she looked around and saw the stars of the night sky.

"Patience!" Daniel shouted from below, having spotted her. "Down here!"

"I'm going to have to jump," she called out to him, stepping carefully toward the edge. "I don't think -"

Before she could finish, she lost her balance again. She stumbled forward and fell, crashing over the edge and quickly tumbling down toward the ground. At the very last second, however, Daniel managed to get beneath her and hold her his arms; she crashed into him, and they both let out pained gasps as they landed together in a mess on the grass. Patience immediately rolled off him, and then as she got her breath back she saw him starting to sit up.

"Nice night for a landing," he stammered.

"Are you trying to impress me?" she asked, stunned that she had finally managed to get out of Hadlow House. She hesitated for a moment, and then she sighed. "Because if you are," she continued, "then I have to tell you, I think it might be working."

EPILOGUE

THE FOLLOWING MORNING, PATIENCE stood in the sewing room of Daniel's father's house – at the back of the yard in the middle of the village – and picked some more dirt and grass from a few cuts on her hand.

"Good morning," a voice said, and she turned to see Daniel standing in the doorway. "I trust you are feeling a little better today?"

"Quite sore," she replied with a faint smile, "but otherwise unharmed. What about you? I am not a light thing to have land on you."

"I'm fine," he said, stepping into the room. "Sore, like you, but I'll recover. I spoke to my father and he completely understands that the situation is difficult. We have room here, so he's happy for you and your father to stay with us for as long as you need."

"I should go and see Father," she told him.

"I believe he's still resting," Daniel explained. "I must confess that, despite the awful nature of everything that happened last night, there is one small positive, and that is that I shall perhaps see a little more of you. Or is it selfish of me to say such a thing?"

"I don't know if it's selfish," she replied, unable to stifle a smile and perhaps even a hint of a blush, "but it is certainly a sentiment that I myself share. And I have to admit that your home is lighter and brighter and far more enjoyable than Hadlow House. Not that I intend to take without giving, of course. While I am here, I am going to work hard and do all the cleaning you could ever need. I can even cook."

"Father will be glad to hear that," he told her. "And Anne too."

"I just want to show my gratitude," she added, as tears glistened in her eyes. "You have no idea how much I appreciate the fact that your father has taken us in."

They stood in silence for a moment, as if neither of them really knew what to say next. Horses could be heard whinnying in the yard, and voices were crying out further off in the village, but both Patience and Daniel seemed unwilling to speak next. After a moment, however, he took her right hand and looked at the cuts across her palm.

"Hadlow House," he said cautiously, "is -"

"Let us speak no more of Hadlow House," she told him firmly. "As far as I am concerned, that place is in the past and we shall never go near it again. I believe that Father, now he is away from its influence, will feel the same way."

"But I still don't quite understand what happened there," he told her. "I confess I am not a man of the world. I have lived my life in Cobblefield and I expect to stay here until my dying day, so there is much I do not know. Indeed, I might even be minded to admit that I am a rather simple man. Still, I wonder whether there is some force out there at that house, some evil that -"

Suddenly Patience stepped forward and kissed him, cutting him off and leaving him in such a startled state that at first he knew not how to respond. The kiss continued for several seconds, however, hovering somewhere between chastity and scandal, before finally Patience pulled back to reveal that she was now blushing more obviously than ever before in her life.

"Right," Daniel said, clearly flustered, "I..."

"I should go and check on Father," she told him, placing a hand on the side of his arm, "but I should like to go for a walk later. I don't know whether you would be interested in accompanying me, but -"

"Yes!" he blurted out, before taking a moment to pull himself together. "I mean... of course, I would be honored to keep you company."

"In about an hour, then," she continued. "Just to the river, perhaps to the little stone bridge. After everything that has happened, I should very much like to try to feel like myself again."

"I shall be ready and waiting," he said with a smile. "Always."

***

Stepping into one of the spare bedrooms upstairs, Patience was surprised to see that her father was not only out of bed, but he had already dressed himself for the day as if he intended to go to work.

"I feel that you might perhaps rest of at least one day," she told him. "How are you feeling this morning, Father?"

"Fine," he murmured. "There is much to do."

"I fear it will do us no good to ignore the events of last night," she replied, choosing in that moment to be a little more forward than before. "Now that we are both away from the influence of that woman, and of that house, we should perhaps discuss what happened." She paused, waiting for an answer, but instead he was busying himself with the last of his ablutions and dress. "I for one do not blame you, Father," she continued, "for anything that occurred. I experienced myself the influence of whatever lingers in that house, and I confess it was almost strong enough to drag me down."

Again she waited. He glanced at her, and she saw the fear in his eyes, but he quickly turned to the table in the corner and began to wipe his gloves clean.

"Mr. Purkiss has been kind enough to let us stay for as long as necessary," she explained. "I don't know if you have had many dealings with him, Father, but -"

"I would rather be alone," he said firmly.

"Father, if -"

"I must consider very carefully what has happened," he added, cutting her off yet again. "You must understand, Patience, that the events of the past few days have been very... distressing for me. Concerning. I must have a full understanding of what occurred before I am able to determine how we should both proceed."

"Of course," she said, trying her very best to remain diplomatic. She took a couple of steps forward. "I would never have left you there," she added. "I would rather have died than leave you at the mercy of that horrible woman. You know..."

She paused, watching the back of his head as he fiddled with something on the table.

"You know that it wasn't Mother, don't

you?" she said softly. "That woman, I know she could be very convincing, but you have to realize that it wasn't Mother. It was some other woman who died a long time ago."

She waited, and after a moment Samuel turned and glared down into her eyes.

"I know it wasn't your mother," he sneered angrily. "Do you take me for a complete fool?"

"Father, no, I just -"

Suddenly she let out a shocked gasp as she felt a pain in her belly. She froze for a moment, meeting her father's gaze, before slowly looking down. To her horror, she saw that he was holding a knife, and that he'd slid that knife directly into her gut. And then, before she had a chance to say anything, he began to slowly twist the blade, causing more and more blood to gush out and start dribbling down onto the floor.

"I always knew that it wasn't your mother," he snarled, leaning closer to her. "And I will not let you, or anyone else, keep me away from her! Do you understand me? I will let no-one stand in my way!"

With that he pulled the knife out. Patience immediately clutched her wound, but blood was flowing between her fingers and after a moment – drained by a sudden weakness – she dropped to her knees. Reaching out, she tried to grab her father's hand for support, but he merely dropped the bloodied knife onto the floor before stepping past her and making his way to the door.

"Father," she stammered, turning and trying once more to reach out to him, "please..."

She watched as he walked out of the room. Once he was gone, she could hear his heavy steps on the stairs. She wanted to go after him, but when she tried to stand she felt her knees buckle. Slumping down, she rolled onto her back and let out a pained gasp as she looked up at the ceiling. She stared at the rippled marks running across the wood, but already her eyes were starting to slip shut.

"Father," she whispered as she began to lose consciousness. "Daniel. Someone... help me..."

As she tried desperately to call out, more and more blood was gushing from her wound, spreading out over her belly and running down her sides to form a growing crimson pool that was even now starting to reach across the room.

***

Once he reached Hadlow House again, Samuel Butler stopped for a moment and looked up at the front door, which had been left open. He hesitated, watching the darkness, and then he walked into the house.

Stopping near the foot of the stairs, he looked around. At first he saw nobody, but after a few seconds he turned and felt cold hands reaching around from behind, running across his chest. And as he heard the soft, soothing whispers of a woman's voice, he smiled and the front door slammed shut.

NEXT IN THIS SERIES

1775

(THE HAUNTING OF HADLOW HOUSE BOOK 3)

Running away isn't always an option. How can a family survive when they're trapped in a haunted house?

Almost one hundred years after tragedy first struck Hadlow House, ghosts still linger in the shadows and threaten to drive the living out of their minds. And some of the house's occupants have never known any other way of life.

Patience desperately wants to escape from the house's oppressive atmosphere. But when she takes refuge in the nearest village, she soon discovers that some ghosts can never be outrun...

1775 is the third book in the *Haunting of Hadlow House* series, which tells the story of one haunted house over the centuries from its construction to the present day. All the lives, all the souls, all the tragedies... and all the ghosts. Readers are advised to start with the first book in the series.

Also by Amy Cross

The Haunting of Nelson Street
(The Ghosts of Crowford book 1)

Crowford, a sleepy coastal town in the south of England, might seem like an oasis of calm and tranquility. Beneath the surface, however, dark secrets are waiting to claim fresh victims, and ghostly figures plot revenge.

Having finally decided to leave the hustle of London, Daisy and Richard Johnson buy two houses on Nelson Street, a picturesque street in the center of Crowford. One house is perfect and ready to move into, while the other is a fire-ravaged wreck that needs a lot of work. They figure they have plenty of time to work on the damaged house while Daisy recovers from a traumatic event.

Soon, they discover that the two houses share a common link to the past. Something awful once happened on Nelson Street, something that shook the town to its core.

Also by Amy Cross

The Revenge of the Mercy Belle
(The Ghosts of Crowford book 2)

The year is 1950, and a great tragedy has struck the town of Crowford. Three local men have been killed in a storm, after their fishing boat the Mercy Belle sank. A mysterious fourth man, however, was rescue. Nobody knows who he is, or what he was doing on the Mercy Belle... and the man has lost his memory.

Five years later, messages from the dead warn of impending doom for Crowford. The ghosts of the Mercy Belle's crew demand revenge, and the whole town is being punished. The fourth man still has no memory of his previous existence, but he's married now and living under the named Edward Smith. As Crowford's suffering continues, the locals begin to turn against him.

What really happened on the night the Mercy Belle sank? Did the fourth man cause the tragedy? And will Crowford survive if this man is not sent to meet his fate?

Also by Amy Cross

The Devil, the Witch and the Whore
(The Deal book 1)

"Leave the forest alone. Whatever's out there, just let it be. Don't make it angry."

When a horrific discovery is made at the edge of town, Sheriff James Kopperud realizes the answers he seeks might be waiting beyond in the vast forest. But everybody in the town of Deal knows that there's something out there in the forest, something that should never be disturbed. A deal was made long ago, a deal that was supposed to keep the town safe. And if he insists on investigating the murder of a local girl, James is going to have to break that deal and head out into the wilderness.

Meanwhile, James has no idea that his estranged daughter Ramsey has returned to town. Ramsey is running from something, and she thinks she can find safety in the vast tunnel system that runs beneath the forest. Before long, however, Ramsey finds herself coming face to face with creatures that hide in the shadows. One of these creatures is known as the devil, and another is known as the witch. They're both waiting for the whore to arrive, but for very different reasons. And soon Ramsey is offered a terrible deal, one that could save or destroy the entire town, and maybe even the world.

Also by Amy Cross

The Soul Auction

"I saw a woman on the beach. I watched her face a demon."

Thirty years after her mother's death, Alice Ashcroft is drawn back to the coastal English town of Curridge. Somebody in Curridge has been reviewing Alice's novels online, and in those reviews there have been tantalizing hints at a hidden truth. A truth that seems to be linked to her dead mother.

"Thirty years ago, there was a soul auction."

Once she reaches Curridge, Alice finds strange things happening all around her. Something attacks her car. A figure watches her on the beach at night. And when she tries to find the person who has been reviewing her books, she makes a horrific discovery.

What really happened to Alice's mother thirty years ago? Who was she talking to, just moments before dropping dead on the beach? What caused a huge rockfall that nearly tore a nearby cliff-face in half? And what sinister presence is lurking in the grounds of the local church?

Also by Amy Cross

Darper Danver: The Complete First Series

Five years ago, three friends went to a remote cabin in the woods and tried to contact the spirit of a long-dead soldier. They thought they could control whatever happened next. They were wrong...

Newly released from prison, Cassie Briggs returns to Fort Powell, determined to get her life back on track. Soon, however, she begins to suspect that an ancient evil still lurks in the nearby cabin. Was the mysterious Darper Danver really destroyed all those years ago, or does her spirit still linger, waiting for a chance to return?

As Cassie and her ex-boyfriend Fisher are finally forced to face the truth about what happened in the cabin, they realize that Darper isn't ready to let go of their lives just yet. Meanwhile, a vengeful woman plots revenge for her brother's murder, and a New York ghost writer arrives in town to uncover the truth. Before long, strange carvings begin to appear around town and blood starts to flow once again.

Also by Amy Cross

The Ghost of Molly Holt

"Molly Holt is dead. There's nothing to fear in this house."

When three teenagers set out to explore an abandoned house in the middle of a forest, they think they've found the location where the infamous Molly Holt video was filmed.

They've found much more than that...

Tim doesn't believe in ghosts, but he has a crush on a girl who does. That's why he ends up taking her out to the house, and it's also why he lets her take his only flashlight. But as they explore the house together, Tim and Becky start to realize that something else might be lurking in the shadows.

Something that, ten years ago, suffered unimaginable pain.

Something that won't rest until a terrible wrong has been put right.

Also by Amy Cross

American Coven

He kidnapped three women and held them in his basement. He thought they couldn't fight back. He was wrong...

Snatched from the street near her home, Holly Carter is taken to a rural house and thrown down into a stone basement. She meets two other women who have also been kidnapped, and soon Holly learns about the horrific rituals that take place in the house. Eventually, she's called upstairs to take her place in the ice bath.

As her nightmare continues, however, Holly learns about a mysterious power that exists in the basement, and which the three women might be able to harness. When they finally manage to get through the metal door, however, the women have no idea that their fight for freedom is going to stretch out for more than a decade, or that it will culminate in a final, devastating demonstration of their new-found powers.

Also by Amy Cross

The Ash House

Why would anyone ever return to a haunted house?

For Diane Mercer the answer is simple. She's dying of cancer, and she wants to know once and for all whether ghosts are real.

Heading home with her young son, Diane is determined to find out whether the stories are real. After all, everyone else claimed to see and hear strange things in the house over the years. Everyone except Diane had some kind of experience in the house, or in the little ash house in the yard.

As Diane explores the house where she grew up, however, her son is exploring the yard and the forest. And while his mother might be struggling to come to terms with her own impending death, Daniel Mercer is puzzled by fleeting appearances of a strange little girl who seems drawn to the ash house, and by strange, rasping coughs that he keeps hearing at night.

The Ash House is a horror novel about a woman who desperately wants to know what will happen to her when she dies, and about a boy who uncovers the shocking truth about a young girl's murder.

Also by Amy Cross

Haunted

Twenty years ago, the ghost of a dead little girl drove Sheriff Michael Blaine to his death.

Now, that same ghost is coming for his daughter.

Returning to the small town where she grew up, Alex Roberts is determined to live a normal, quiet life. For the residents of Railham, however, she's an unwelcome reminder of the town's darkest hour.

Twenty years ago, nine-year-old Mo Garvey was found brutally murdered in a nearby forest. Everyone thinks that Alex's father was responsible, but if the killer was brought to justice, why is the ghost of Mo Garvey still after revenge?

And how far will the real killer go to protect his secret, when Alex starts getting closer to the truth?

Haunted is a horror novel about a woman who has to face her past, about a town that would rather forget, and about a little girl who refuses to let death stand in her way.

Also by Amy Cross

The Curse of Wetherley House

"If you walk through that door, Evil Mary will get you."

When she agrees to visit a supposedly haunted house with an old friend, Rosie assumes she'll encounter nothing more scary than a few creaks and bumps in the night. Even the legend of Evil Mary doesn't put her off. After all, she knows ghosts aren't real. But when Mary makes her first appearance, Rosie realizes she might already be trapped.

For more than a century, Wetherley House has been cursed. A horrific encounter on a remote road in the late 1800's has already caused a chain of misery and pain for all those who live at the house. Wetherley House was abandoned long ago, after a terrible discovery in the basement, something has remained undetected within its room. And even the local children know that Evil Mary waits in the house for anyone foolish enough to walk through the front door.

Before long, Rosie realizes that her entire life has been defined by the spirit of a woman who died in agony. Can she become the first person to escape Evil Mary, or will she fall victim to the same fate as the house's other occupants?

Also by Amy Cross

The Ghosts of Hexley Airport

Ten years ago, more than two hundred people died in a horrific plane crash at Hexley Airport.

Today, some say their ghosts still haunt the terminal building.

When she starts her new job at the airport, working a night shift as part of the security team, Casey assumes the stories about the place can't be true. Even when she has a strange encounter in a deserted part of the departure hall, she's certain that ghosts aren't real.

Soon, however, she's forced to face the truth. Not only is there something haunting the airport's buildings and tarmac, but a sinister force is working behind the scenes to replicate the circumstances of the original accident. And as a snowstorm moves in, Hexley Airport looks set to witness yet another disaster.

Also by Amy Cross

The Girl Who Never Came Back

Twenty years ago, Charlotte Abernathy vanished while playing near her family's house. Despite a frantic search, no trace of her was found until a year later, when the little girl turned up on the doorstep with no memory of where she'd been.

Today, Charlotte has put her mysterious ordeal behind her, even though she's never learned where she was during that missing year. However, when her eight-year-old niece vanishes in similar circumstances, a fully-grown Charlotte is forced to make a fresh attempt to uncover the truth.

Originally published in 2013, the fully revised and updated version of *The Girl Who Never Came Back* tells the harrowing story of a woman who thought she could forget her past, and of a little girl caught in the tangled web of a dark family secret.

Also by Amy Cross

Asylum
(The Asylum Trilogy book 1)

"No-one ever leaves Lakehurst. The staff, the patients, the ghosts... Once you're here, you're stuck forever."

After shooting her little brother dead, Annie Radford is sent to Lakehurst psychiatric hospital for assessment. Hearing voices in her head, Annie is forced to undergo experimental new treatments devised by a mysterious old man who lives in the hospital's attic. It soon becomes clear that the hospital's staff, led by the vicious Nurse Winter, are hiding something horrific at Lakehurst.

As Annie struggles to survive the hospital, she learns more about Nurse Winter's own story. Once a promising young medical student, Kirsten Winter also heard voices in her head. Voices that traveled a long way to reach her. Voices that have a plan of their own. Voices that will stop at nothing to get what they want.

What kind of signals are being transmitted from the basement of the hospital? Who is the old man in the attic? Why are living human brains kept in jars? And what is the dark secret that lurks at the heart of the hospital?

BOOKS BY AMY CROSS

1. Dark Season: The Complete First Series (2011)
2. Werewolves of Soho (Lupine Howl book 1) (2012)
3. Werewolves of the Other London (Lupine Howl book 2) (2012)
4. Ghosts: The Complete Series (2012)
5. Dark Season: The Complete Second Series (2012)
6. The Children of Black Annis (Lupine Howl book 3) (2012)
7. Destiny of the Last Wolf (Lupine Howl book 4) (2012)
8. Asylum (The Asylum Trilogy book 1) (2012)
9. Dark Season: The Complete Third Series (2013)
10. Devil's Briar (2013)
11. Broken Blue (The Broken Trilogy book 1) (2013)
12. The Night Girl (2013)
13. Days 1 to 4 (Mass Extinction Event book 1) (2013)
14. Days 5 to 8 (Mass Extinction Event book 2) (2013)
15. The Library (The Library Chronicles book 1) (2013)
16. American Coven (2013)
17. Werewolves of Sangreth (Lupine Howl book 5) (2013)
18. Broken White (The Broken Trilogy book 2) (2013)
19. Grave Girl (Grave Girl book 1) (2013)
20. Other People's Bodies (2013)
21. The Shades (2013)
22. The Vampire's Grave and Other Stories (2013)
23. Darper Danver: The Complete First Series (2013)
24. The Hollow Church (2013)
25. The Dead and the Dying (2013)
26. Days 9 to 16 (Mass Extinction Event book 3) (2013)
27. The Girl Who Never Came Back (2013)
28. Ward Z (The Ward Z Series book 1) (2013)
29. Journey to the Library (The Library Chronicles book 2) (2014)
30. The Vampires of Tor Cliff Asylum (2014)
31. The Family Man (2014)
32. The Devil's Blade (2014)
33. The Immortal Wolf (Lupine Howl book 6) (2014)
34. The Dying Streets (Detective Laura Foster book 1) (2014)
35. The Stars My Home (2014)
36. The Ghost in the Rain and Other Stories (2014)
37. Ghosts of the River Thames (The Robinson Chronicles book 1) (2014)
38. The Wolves of Cur'eath (2014)
39. Days 46 to 53 (Mass Extinction Event book 4) (2014)
40. The Man Who Saw the Face of the World (2014)

41. The Art of Dying (Detective Laura Foster book 2) (2014)
42. Raven Revivals (Grave Girl book 2) (2014)
43. Arrival on Thaxos (Dead Souls book 1) (2014)
44. Birthright (Dead Souls book 2) (2014)
45. A Man of Ghosts (Dead Souls book 3) (2014)
46. The Haunting of Hardstone Jail (2014)
47. A Very Respectable Woman (2015)
48. Better the Devil (2015)
49. The Haunting of Marshall Heights (2015)
50. Terror at Camp Everbee (The Ward Z Series book 2) (2015)
51. Guided by Evil (Dead Souls book 4) (2015)
52. Child of a Bloodied Hand (Dead Souls book 5) (2015)
53. Promises of the Dead (Dead Souls book 6) (2015)
54. Days 54 to 61 (Mass Extinction Event book 5) (2015)
55. Angels in the Machine (The Robinson Chronicles book 2) (2015)
56. The Curse of Ah-Qal's Tomb (2015)
57. Broken Red (The Broken Trilogy book 3) (2015)
58. The Farm (2015)
59. Fallen Heroes (Detective Laura Foster book 3) (2015)
60. The Haunting of Emily Stone (2015)
61. Cursed Across Time (Dead Souls book 7) (2015)
62. Destiny of the Dead (Dead Souls book 8) (2015)
63. The Death of Jennifer Kazakos (Dead Souls book 9) (2015)
64. Alice Isn't Well (Death Herself book 1) (2015)
65. Annie's Room (2015)
66. The House on Everley Street (Death Herself book 2) (2015)
67. Meds (The Asylum Trilogy book 2) (2015)
68. Take Me to Church (2015)
69. Ascension (Demon's Grail book 1) (2015)
70. The Priest Hole (Nykolas Freeman book 1) (2015)
71. Eli's Town (2015)
72. The Horror of Raven's Briar Orphanage (Dead Souls book 10) (2015)
73. The Witch of Thaxos (Dead Souls book 11) (2015)
74. The Rise of Ashalla (Dead Souls book 12) (2015)
75. Evolution (Demon's Grail book 2) (2015)
76. The Island (The Island book 1) (2015)
77. The Lighthouse (2015)
78. The Cabin (The Cabin Trilogy book 1) (2015)
79. At the Edge of the Forest (2015)
80. The Devil's Hand (2015)
81. The 13th Demon (Demon's Grail book 3) (2016)
82. After the Cabin (The Cabin Trilogy book 2) (2016)
83. The Border: The Complete Series (2016)
84. The Dead Ones (Death Herself book 3) (2016)

85. A House in London (2016)
86. Persona (The Island book 2) (2016)
87. Battlefield (Nykolas Freeman book 2) (2016)
88. Perfect Little Monsters and Other Stories (2016)
89. The Ghost of Shapley Hall (2016)
90. The Blood House (2016)
91. The Death of Addie Gray (2016)
92. The Girl With Crooked Fangs (2016)
93. Last Wrong Turn (2016)
94. The Body at Auercliff (2016)
95. The Printer From Hell (2016)
96. The Dog (2016)
97. The Nurse (2016)
98. The Haunting of Blackwych Grange (2016)
99. Twisted Little Things and Other Stories (2016)
100. The Horror of Devil's Root Lake (2016)
101. The Disappearance of Katie Wren (2016)
102. B&B (2016)
103. The Bride of Ashbyrn House (2016)
104. The Devil, the Witch and the Whore (The Deal Trilogy book 1) (2016)
105. The Ghosts of Lakeforth Hotel (2016)
106. The Ghost of Longthorn Manor and Other Stories (2016)
107. Laura (2017)
108. The Murder at Skellin Cottage (Jo Mason book 1) (2017)
109. The Curse of Wetherley House (2017)
110. The Ghosts of Hexley Airport (2017)
111. The Return of Rachel Stone (Jo Mason book 2) (2017)
112. Haunted (2017)
113. The Vampire of Downing Street and Other Stories (2017)
114. The Ash House (2017)
115. The Ghost of Molly Holt (2017)
116. The Camera Man (2017)
117. The Soul Auction (2017)
118. The Abyss (The Island book 3) (2017)
119. Broken Window (The House of Jack the Ripper book 1) (2017)
120. In Darkness Dwell (The House of Jack the Ripper book 2) (2017)
121. Cradle to Grave (The House of Jack the Ripper book 3) (2017)
122. The Lady Screams (The House of Jack the Ripper book 4) (2017)
123. A Beast Well Tamed (The House of Jack the Ripper book 5) (2017)
124. Doctor Charles Grazier (The House of Jack the Ripper book 6) (2017)
125. The Raven Watcher (The House of Jack the Ripper book 7) (2017)
126. The Final Act (The House of Jack the Ripper book 8) (2017)
127. Stephen (2017)
128. The Spider (2017)

129. The Mermaid's Revenge (2017)
130. The Girl Who Threw Rocks at the Devil (2018)
131. Friend From the Internet (2018)
132. Beautiful Familiar (2018)
133. One Night at a Soul Auction (2018)
134. 16 Frames of the Devil's Face (2018)
135. The Haunting of Caldgrave House (2018)
136. Like Stones on a Crow's Back (The Deal Trilogy book 2) (2018)
137. Room 9 and Other Stories (2018)
138. The Gravest Girl of All (Grave Girl book 3) (2018)
139. Return to Thaxos (Dead Souls book 13) (2018)
140. The Madness of Annie Radford (The Asylum Trilogy book 3) (2018)
141. The Haunting of Briarwych Church (Briarwych book 1) (2018)
142. I Just Want You To Be Happy (2018)
143. Day 100 (Mass Extinction Event book 6) (2018)
144. The Horror of Briarwych Church (Briarwych book 2) (2018)
145. The Ghost of Briarwych Church (Briarwych book 3) (2018)
146. Lights Out (2019)
147. Apocalypse (The Ward Z Series book 3) (2019)
148. Days 101 to 108 (Mass Extinction Event book 7) (2019)
149. The Haunting of Daniel Bayliss (2019)
150. The Purchase (2019)
151. Harper's Hotel Ghost Girl (Death Herself book 4) (2019)
152. The Haunting of Aldburn House (2019)
153. Days 109 to 116 (Mass Extinction Event book 8) (2019)
154. Bad News (2019)
155. The Wedding of Rachel Blaine (2019)
156. Dark Little Wonders and Other Stories (2019)
157. The Music Man (2019)
158. The Vampire Falls (Three Nights of the Vampire book 1) (2019)
159. The Other Ann (2019)
160. The Butcher's Husband and Other Stories (2019)
161. The Haunting of Lannister Hall (2019)
162. The Vampire Burns (Three Nights of the Vampire book 2) (2019)
163. Days 195 to 202 (Mass Extinction Event book 9) (2019)
164. Escape From Hotel Necro (2019)
165. The Vampire Rises (Three Nights of the Vampire book 3) (2019)
166. Ten Chimes to Midnight: A Collection of Ghost Stories (2019)
167. The Strangler's Daughter (2019)
168. The Beast on the Tracks (2019)
169. The Haunting of the King's Head (2019)
170. I Married a Serial Killer (2019)
171. Your Inhuman Heart (2020)
172. Days 203 to 210 (Mass Extinction Event book 10) (2020)

173. The Ghosts of David Brook (2020)
174. Days 349 to 356 (Mass Extinction Event book 11) (2020)
175. The Horror at Criven Farm (2020)
176. Mary (2020)
177. The Middlewych Experiment (Chaos Gear Annie book 1) (2020)
178. Days 357 to 364 (Mass Extinction Event book 12) (2020)
179. Day 365: The Final Day (Mass Extinction Event book 13) (2020)
180. The Haunting of Hathaway House (2020)
181. Don't Let the Devil Know Your Name (2020)
182. The Legend of Rinth (2020)
183. The Ghost of Old Coal House (2020)
184. The Root (2020)
185. I'm Not a Zombie (2020)
186. The Ghost of Annie Close (2020)
187. The Disappearance of Lonnie James (2020)
188. The Curse of the Langfords (2020)
189. The Haunting of Nelson Street (The Ghosts of Crowford 1) (2020)
190. Strange Little Horrors and Other Stories (2020)
191. The House Where She Died (2020)
192. The Revenge of the Mercy Belle (The Ghosts of Crowford 2) (2020)
193. The Ghost of Crowford School (The Ghosts of Crowford book 3) (2020)
194. The Haunting of Hardlocke House (2020)
195. The Cemetery Ghost (2020)
196. You Should Have Seen Her (2020)
197. The Portrait of Sister Elsa (The Ghosts of Crowford book 4) (2021)
198. The House on Fisher Street (2021)
199. The Haunting of the Crowford Hoy (The Ghosts of Crowford 5) (2021)
200. Trill (2021)
201. The Horror of the Crowford Empire (The Ghosts of Crowford 6) (2021)
202. Out There (The Ted Armitage Trilogy book 1) (2021)
203. The Nightmare of Crowford Hospital (The Ghosts of Crowford 7) (2021)
204. Twist Valley (The Ted Armitage Trilogy book 2) (2021)
205. The Great Beyond (The Ted Armitage Trilogy book 3) (2021)
206. The Haunting of Edward House (2021)
207. The Curse of the Crowford Grand (The Ghosts of Crowford 8) (2021)
208. How to Make a Ghost (2021)
209. The Ghosts of Crossley Manor (The Ghosts of Crowford 9) (2021)
210. The Haunting of Matthew Thorne (2021)
211. The Siege of Crowford Castle (The Ghosts of Crowford 10) (2021)
212. Daisy: The Complete Series (2021)
213. Bait (Bait book 1) (2021)
214. Origin (Bait book 2) (2021)
215. Heretic (Bait book 3) (2021)
216. Anna's Sister (2021)

217. The Haunting of Quist House (The Rose Files 1) (2021)
218. The Haunting of Crowford Station (The Ghosts of Crowford 11) (2022)
219. The Curse of Rosie Stone (2022)
220. The First Order (The Chronicles of Sister June book 1) (2022)
221. The Second Veil (The Chronicles of Sister June book 2) (2022)
222. The Graves of Crowford Rise (The Ghosts of Crowford 12) (2022)
223. Dead Man: The Resurrection of Morton Kane (2022)
224. The Third Beast (The Chronicles of Sister June book 3) (2022)
225. The Legend of the Crossley Stag (The Ghosts of Crowford 13) (2022)
226. One Star (2022)
227. The Ghost in Room 119 (2022)
228. The Fourth Shadow (The Chronicles of Sister June book 4) (2022)
229. The Soldier Without a Past (Dead Souls book 14) (2022)
230. The Ghosts of Marsh House (2022)
231. Wax: The Complete Series (2022)
232. The Phantom of Crowford Theatre (The Ghosts of Crowford 14) (2022)
233. The Haunting of Hurst House (Mercy Willow book 1) (2022)
234. Blood Rains Down From the Sky (The Deal Trilogy book 3) (2022)
235. The Spirit on Sidle Street (Mercy Willow book 2) (2022)
236. The Ghost of Gower Grange (Mercy Willow book 3) (2022)
237. The Curse of Clute Cottage (Mercy Willow book 4) (2022)
238. The Haunting of Anna Jenkins (Mercy Willow book 5) (2023)
239. The Death of Mercy Willow (Mercy Willow book 6) (2023)
240. Angel (2023)
241. The Eyes of Maddy Park (2023)
242. If You Didn't Like Me Then, You Probably Won't Like Me Now (2023)
243. The Terror of Torfork Tower (Mercy Willow 7) (2023)
244. The Phantom of Payne Priory (Mercy Willow 8) (2023)
245. The Devil on Davis Drive (Mercy Willow 9) (2023)
246. The Haunting of the Ghost of Tom Bell (Mercy Willow 10) (2023)
247. The Other Ghost of Gower Grange (Mercy Willow 11) (2023)
248. The Haunting of Olive Atkins (Mercy Willow 12) (2023)
249. The End of Marcy Willow (Mercy Willow 13) (2023)
250. The Last Haunted House on Mars and Other Stories (2023)

For more information, visit:

www.amycross.com

Printed in Great Britain
by Amazon